THE SCYTHE

Balogun Ojetade

ISBN-10:099140730X
ISBN-13:9780991407309

DEDICATION

I dedicate this book to Donald Goines, Walter Mosley, Charles R. Saunders and Derrick Ferguson, all great Black Pulp authors who continue to inspire me to write Pulp through their works and have made me continue to love this amazing genre.

And to my father, who is now my muse and my guide from the other side of the veil. May the Ancestors and his Comrades in Heaven – be very pleased with him.

ACKNOWLEDGMENTS

I would like to thank my wife, Iyalogun Ojetade for being so supportive and patient as I continue my mission to bring the world the best in Black Speculative Fiction.
I would also like to thank Milton Davis, Maurice Broaddus, Valjeanne Jeffers and all the other up-and-coming Steamfunk authors for helping to keep the Steamfunk movement alive.

CHAPTER ONE

March 23, 1921

Dr. A.C. Jackson stepped off the train at the Frisco Railroad Yard onto the moist stone platform. He closed his eyes and inhaled, relishing the fresh, green smell of Tulsa rain. Spring was Dr. Jackson's favorite time of year. He loved the rain; the cool winds; even the occasional tornadoes.

"Dr. Jackson," a voice called behind him. *"Dr. A.C. Jackson?"*

The doctor turned toward the voice.

Standing before him was a man in his mid-thirties, several years younger than Dr. Jackson. Standing beside the man was a boy of about twelve or thirteen years old. The boy's suit, consisting of a pristine white shirt, navy blue bow tie, navy blue jacket and matching shorts and a navy blue page-boy hat matched his father's navy blue, wool three-piece. The man held a folded newspaper in his ebony hand.

"Yes, I'm he," Dr. Jackson, replied. "How can I help you, sir?"

The man extended his right hand. "My name's Ozzie Parker, sir. My son, here is Ozzie, Junior."

Dr. Jackson shook Ozzie's hand. "Pleased to meet you, Mr. Parker. Hey, there, Junior."

"Hi, Mr. Doctor, sir," Ozzie stuttered.

"Junior is going to be a doctor when he grows up," Ozzie said. "A surgeon, like you. Ain't that right, Junior?"

"Yes, sir," Junior replied.

Ozzie unfolded the newspaper – the *Tulsa Star*. A photograph of Dr. Jackson, standing in front of his practice on Greenwood Avenue in his white lab coat, graced the front page. The headline above the photo read *"Famed Dr. William Mayo calls Dr. A.C. Jackson 'the most able Negro surgeon in America!'"*

The headlines were true. William Mayo had, indeed, said that. What did not make headlines, however, was when William Mayo's father, W.W. Mayo – an even more accomplished surgeon – corrected William and said *"No, Dr. A.C. Jackson is the most able surgeon in America, Negro or otherwise."*

"Would you please autograph this for him?" Ozzie said, pointing toward the newspaper. "He's shy, but it'd mean a lot to him."

"Absolutely," Dr. Jackson said, squatting beside his suitcase. "I'll just retrieve a pencil from my suitcase."

"I have a pen, sir," Ozzie said, reaching into his pocket and retrieving a crimson, *Parker Duofold* fountain pen.

Dr. Jackson stood and reached for the pen.

Ozzie handed it to him.

Dr. Jackson whistled, examining the pen with his thin, russet-colored fingers. "The 'Big Red'...this is a fine piece of work, Mr. Parker. How much did this run you? Six...seven dollars?"

"Nothing, sir," Ozzie replied. "George Safford Parker is my grandfather. I'm opening a pen and paper shop down on Greenwood Avenue. The Duofold is going to be our featured item."

Dr. Jackson scribbled his signature across his photograph. "My clinic is down on Greenwood. Come see me once you get settled in and I'll take you around and introduce you to some folks you should know."

"Thank you, Dr. Jackson," Ozzie said. "Oh, and keep the pen as a token of my appreciation.

"Thank you, Mr. Parker," Dr. Jackson said.

"I'll see you soon," Ozzie said. "Come on, Junior."

"Goodbye, Junior," Dr. Jackson said, waving at the boy.

Bye, sir," Junior replied, walking behind his father.

Dr. Jackson picked up his suitcase and walked to the corner to await the next taxi. A smile spread across his face. He was happy to be back in Tulsa and could not wait to be back at his office – and among all the hustle and bustle typical of

Greenwood Avenue. The booming business district was commonly known as *'Negro Wallstreet'* because of all of the successful, black-owned businesses, run by wealthy business owners, on that street in the Black area of Tulsa.

Greenwood Avenue was the envy of all Tulsa and was the city's most important street, because it ran north for over a mile from the Frisco Railroad Yards, and it was one of the few streets that did not cross through both Black and white neighborhoods. The citizens of Greenwood took pride in this fact because it was something they had all to themselves and did not have to share with the white community of Tulsa.

Dr. Jackson tapped his feet rapidly and then whirled about. He looked skyward and crooned his favorite song:

"When life seems full of clouds and rain,
And I am full of nothin' and pain
Who soothes my thumpin', bumpin' brain?
Umm...
Nobody!
When winter comes with snow and

sleet

And me with hunger and cold feet

Who says, 'Here's twenty-five cents, go ahead and get somethin' to eat?'

Nobody!

I ain't never done nothin' to nobody...

I ain't never done nothin' to nobody, no time...

So until I get somethin' from somebody sometime,

I'll never do nothin' for nobody, no time."

###

May 31, 1921

"Dr. Jackson, come quickly!"

Dr. Jackson dashed into Examination Room Four. His assistant of three years, nurse Rita McCray, crouched by the window. Her face was a mask of fear and shock. "What is it, Rita? What's wrong?"

"Those rubes have Ozzie Parker surrounded in the street!" Nurse McCray cried.

"What?" Dr. Jackson gasped, running to the window.

He knelt beside Rita and peered over the window sill.

Four white men – their clothes and boots spotted with dirt and splashes of blood – surrounded Ozzie. His grey, three-piece suit was torn at the right shoulder and a patch of dirt, in the shape of a boot, stained the back of his suit coat. Ozzie thrust a Duofold in front of him in an attempt to keep his attackers at bay.

"I'm going out there," Dr. Jackson said, leaping to his feet.

Rita grabbed his wrist and held his hand to her chest. "Dr. Jackson, don't! You'll just get yourself killed."

"I have to do *something*," Dr. Jackson said.

"Look out there," Rita said, thrusting her finger toward the window. "The movie theater...my brother's grocery store...the hospital...all on fire! Those devils have brought Hell to Greenwood. The best we can do now is lay low until this all blows over."

This madness isn't likely to ever blow over, Dr. Jackson thought.

The violence erupted after seventeen-year old, white elevator operator, Sarah Page, accused nineteen-year old Dick Rowland – a Black man – of assault.

Dick Rowland was cleared of the charge, which sent the white residents of Tulsa into a frenzy and shortly after, there was news that a white lynch mob was going to take matters into its own hands and kill Dick Rowland.

A group of armed white men congregated outside the jail prior to Rowland's release.

In response, a group of Black men joined the assembled crowd in order to protect Dick Rowland. Tempers flared; guns were fired...

And Hell fell upon Greenwood.

An agonized scream tore across the blackened sky.

Dr. Jackson looked out the window in time to see Ozzie fall to the ground, blood pouring from a gaping wound in the side of his head.

Dr. Jackson slid down the wall and collapsed onto his haunches. "Damn, too late. Ozzie is..."

"I know," Rita sobbed. "Ozzie was a good..."

"His son!" Dr. Jackson wailed. "I have to see if Ozzie Junior is okay."

"Dr. Jackson," Rita sighed. "You already know that boy is gone."

Dr. Jackson smacked the sides of his head with his palms. "I..."

A loud knock on the front door made them both jump.

Dr. Jackson slowly rose to his feet. "Who?"

"Don't go to the door," Rita whispered.

"I have to," Dr. Jackson replied. "Someone might need my help. It could be Junior."

He scurried out, crept past the other examination rooms and then tip-toed toward the door.

Another knock – this one stronger than the first – shook the mahogany door.

"Who is it?" Dr. Jackson called.

"My friend here is hurt and needs some medicine," a nasal voice replied.

"You don't sound like a negro," Dr. Jackson said.

"You don't either, boy," the man on the other side of the door snickered.

"Please, go away," Dr. Jackson shouted.

"Look, just give us some bandages and some medicine for pain and we'll leave you and your place untouched," the man replied. "We ain't gonna hurt you, boy. Now open up!"

"Hold on," Dr. Jackson said as he ran to a metal cabinet behind the receptionist's desk. He yanked the cabinet door open and then withdrew two rolls of cloth bandages and a small jar filled with an amber cream.

Rita crawled out of the examination room.

Dr. Jackson waved his hand toward the room as he shook his head. "Hide!"

Rita scurried back into Examination Room Four.

Dr. Jackson unlocked the front door and then opened it. He stepped outside and closed the door behind him.

Standing before the doctor were two men.

One, he recognized from the *Tulsa Star* newspaper as Earl May, owner of *May's Masks*, who was recently exonerated of the rape of a nine year old black girl.

The other man, while dressed in soiled overalls and reeking of alcohol and sweat like Earl May, seemed out of place. His brunette hair was immaculately groomed, his teeth were perfectly straight and there was not one blemish on his tan skin.

Neither man appeared to be injured at all.

Dr. Jackson stretched out his arms, offering the medical supplies to Earl May. "Here you go. The salve is my own concoction; a mixture of arnica, camphor and brandy."

"Now, that's a shine for you," the well-groomed man chuckled. "Smart *and* stupid all at the same time."

"What?" Dr. Jackson inquired.

Earl May leered at Dr. Jackson, a crooked smile spread across his ruddy face.

Doctor Jackson felt like a rabbit that had just burrowed into a den of foxes.

"You should have stayed inside, boy," Earl May said.

Dr. Jackson tossed the bandages and salve into Earl May's face and then spun on his heels. He darted toward the door.

A loud boom rent the air.

A searing pain gnawed its way through the doctor's calf.

Dr. Jackson collapsed onto his left knee.

A second shot struck Dr. Jackson's lower back. He collapsed onto his side.

The doctor rolled onto his back, desperately grasping at consciousness yet feeling it slip between his fingers – as slick as the blood rapidly spreading across his doorway.

The well-groomed man stomped down onto Dr. Jackson's chest, grinding the heel of his boot into the doctor's solar plexus. "Do shines go to the same Hell as the white man? Write me and let me know."

Fire erupted from the muzzle of the well-groomed man's revolver.

Waves of darkness and silence swept over the good doctor. His vision faded...his heart fluttered. He was gone from this world – taken, by the waves, to the land of Forever-Night.

CHAPTER TWO

MAY 31, 1921

A.C. Jackson awakened in moist blackness and blistering heat.

A small light, the size of the head of a pin, floated in the darkness, flitting about like a bee in a field of roses.

"Is this...Heaven?" Dr. Jackson whispered.

"*No, it is not.*"

The voice was soft, yet strong, like a brass dinner bell. It did not, however, ring in his ears, but in the depths of his mind.

Dr. Jackson swallowed hard. "Hell, then?"

A soothing chime rang in his head. The rhythm and tone of the chime gave Dr. Jackson the feeling that the bell-voice was giggling.

"Not Hell, either," the chiming voice sang. "You are at the crossroad between the realm of the Quick and that of the Dead."

"And where are you?" Dr. Jackson said. "Please, show yourself."

"Do you not see me?" The voice inquired. "Here, let me come a bit closer."

The miniscule point of light flew toward Dr. Jackson until he could finally make out its shape.

"You're a...a..."

"A scythe," the voice chimed. "*The* scythe, actually. My name is Ikukulu."

"*The* scythe?" Dr. Jackson inquired, echoing Ikukulu.

"Of Death," Ikukulu answered.

"And you talk?"

"If not, you're insane; you *are* holding a conversation with me, after all," Ikukulu replied.

"True," Dr. Jackson said, nodding in agreement. "So, am I dead?"

"Very," Ikukulu answered. "However, I brought you here to offer you a second chance at life."

"How? Why?" Dr. Jackson asked.

"When I venture out with my master to gather the dead, I am always amazed – and somewhat puzzled, I must admit – by the struggle you mortals put up to stay alive," Ikukulu replied. "Life and Death are merely phases of existence, yet you cling to Life as if it is the most precious thing in creation. I want to experience Life in the way you do in hopes that I might one day understand."

"And just what do you need me for?"

"I want to become one with your Ori Inu – your subconscious mind," Ikukulu replied. "Doing so will allow me to feel what you feel; do what you do; be who you are. In exchange, I will grant you life...and a portion of my power, so you can avenge your death and the deaths of all those people in the Greenwood neighborhood of Tulsa, Oklahoma."

"How?"

"Just agree and I will return you to the realm of the Quick posthaste."

"I...I agree," Dr. Jackson whispered.

"Excellent!" Ikukulu sang.

The tiny scythe flew into the gaping gunshot wound in Dr. Jackson's skull.

###

June 1, 1921

A cold, white light fell over Dr. Jackson like a blanket. He felt himself moving through something thick, gummy and dank.

A moment later, he was on his knees in the doorway of the torched remains of his practice.

Dr. Jackson pulled himself to his feet and perused his surroundings. Most of the shops, churches and schools were burned to the ground. The sky was black with smoke and great craters dotted the streets. Not one living soul – besides the doctor – was anywhere to be seen.

His pained lamentations were devoured by the charred sky.

Dr. Jackson sprinted across the street toward where *West's Funeral*

Home used to sit. He stopped at a chocolate-colored hearse that was parked in the driveway and peeked through the driver's window. The key was in the ignition, where old man West always left it.

Dr. Jackson opened the driver's door, catching a quick glimpse of himself in the lantern mounted on the side of the hearse. He snapped his head toward the lantern and stared – in shock – at his reflection. The bullet wound in his forehead was closed and not even a scar was evident. He appeared to be twenty years younger than his forty-six years of age and his salt-and-pepper hair was now jet-black.

He rubbed his fingers across his smooth cheeks, shaking his head in disbelief. *A second chance at life, indeed.*

Dr. Jackson slid into the driver's seat of the hearse and turned the key. The car coughed and spat in protest and then came to life.

He hit the accelerator and the hearse sped off, leaving behind his beloved *'Negro Wall Street.'*

###

Dr. Jackson brought the hearse to a stop across the street from *May's Masks*.

The street was quiet. The smell of baked bread, engine oil and iron assaulted his nostrils.

He crept toward the dimly lit mask shop. When he was within a foot of the door, he felt a slight tug on his insides, as if his internal organs were being pulled by lines of fishing wire. He did not resist the pull as it grew stronger, the pull becoming a hard yank.

And then he vanished in a cloud of dirt, which reeked of decay, mildew and muck.

A moment later, he reappeared inside of Earl May's shop.

The corners of Dr. Jackson's mouth curled upward into a smile. Thanks to Ikukulu – the Scythe – he now had power and he was eager to show Earl May just how much.

A low, clanking noise issued from the back room.

Dr. Jackson crept toward the sound until before him sat Earl May, pounding away at a Death's-head mask formed of tin.

Lost in his work and with his back to Dr. Jackson, May took no notice as the doctor sauntered toward him.

"Nice work," Dr. Jackson whispered.

May leapt to his feet and turned to face Dr. Jackson with his hammer raised high above his head. "Who the hell?"

"I'm the doctor who offered you a balm for your pain," Dr. Jackson replied. "Now I just offer you pain."

May's eyes widened and his jaw fell slack as he realized who the man standing before him – his suit caked in blood and reeking of death – really was..

"No...it can't be!" May screamed. "You don't look like him...besides, we...we killed you...*him*!"

Earl May brought the hammer down.

Doctor Jackson raised his arm to block the blow.

The hammer slammed into the doctor's forearm with a loud crack.

The head of the hammer flew across the room as the hammer's haft shattered.

To Dr. Jackson, the strike felt no more bothersome than a blow from a rolled up newspaper.

The doctor countered with a strike of his own, his fist slamming into Earl May's chest like a cannonball.

The mask maker slid backward, coming to an abrupt stop when his back collided with the wall behind him.

May collapsed onto his knees, clutching at his chest as he struggled to suck in quick, erratic breaths between his slack and drooling lips.

"Can't breathe, eh?" Dr. Jackson said as he crept toward Earl May. "Your sternum is fractured. Tell me the name of the man who shot me in the head and I'll fix you right up."

May lowered his gaze. A line of spittle fell onto his lap.

Dr. Jackson drove his knee into May's biceps.

May screamed in agony as the bones in his upper arm shattered from the pulverizing force of the blow.

"I will break every bone in your boorish body if you don't tell me the man's name right now."

"Okay, okay!" May cried. "He's my cousin...lives in Atlanta, Georgia..."

"His name!" Dr. Jackson hissed.

"Woodruff," Earl May sobbed. "Ernest Woodruff."

CHAPTER THREE

September 5, 1922

"Now ain't this a kick in the head?"

A beautiful woman, with cocoa skin and a strut like a lioness on the hunt, stormed into the doctor's office.

"What's wrong, Marie?" He asked.

"That Scythe cat hit another Coca-Cola truck, Dr. Cygnet," she replied, calling Dr. Jackson by the name he had worn since relocating to Atlanta a little over a year ago.

He had taken his mother's maiden name and his father's middle name.

A new name for a new man, he had told himself.

"Scythe?" the doctor inquired, feigning ignorance.

"That's what all the newspapers are calling him," Marie replied. "He keeps sabotaging Coca-Cola shipments, setting the trucks on fire...terrorizing the drivers. Deliveries to pharmacies are late as hell. I ordered a crate a week ago and still haven't gotten it."

Marie's curly, black hair danced upon her shoulders as she shook her head. "I can't run a pharmacy without Coca-Cola! Applesauce!"

"Negroes need to get together and we make our own fountain drink," Dr. 'Cygnet' said.

"Ernest Woodruff would burn Auburn Avenue to the ground if we tried that," Marie said. "There wouldn't be a...applesauce! I am so sorry, Dr. Cygnet."

"It's okay," Dr. Cygnet replied.

"No, it's not," Marie sighed, lowering her gaze. "After all you went through in Tulsa...I should have been more sensitive to that."

"If you didn't speak your mind, you wouldn't be *you*, Marie Lefleur," Dr. Cygnet said, gently raising her chin with the tips of his fingers. "Don't change that; it's one of the things everyone loves about you."

The doctor kissed Marie on the forehead.

Marie's cheeks reddened. "Well, ain't you the bee's knees?!"

"*And* the cat's meow," Dr. Cygnet said, walking toward the door. "And for the hundredth time, call me Jerry...we're partners."

"Negro doctors don't get the recognition they deserve," Marie said. "So, I want the world to give you your due. Besides, one day, you're gonna be my husband, so I wanna show you off."

"Your husband?" Dr. Cygnet chuckled. "We haven't even gone out to dinner yet."

"I guess we'd better do something about that, then," Marie said.

"How about this Friday? Dr. Cygnet asked. "At the Municipal Market?"

"It's a date," Marie replied.

Dr. Cygnet nodded, tossed his fedora onto his head and stepped a foot out of the door. "I have a house-call; if it runs long, I will see you in the morning."

"Be safe, Doc'," Marie said.

"Always," Dr. Cygnet replied as he left the office. "Safer than Citizen's Trust."

###

The night air was muggy; warm. But the heart of the man sitting at the wheel of the chocolate-colored hearse was cold. As cold as the grave.

He slid the tin Death's-head mask he had taken from Earl May's shop – now tarnished a dull grey – onto his face. The mask shifted, liquefied and then molded to Dr. Cygnet's face, transforming his handsome visage into a twisted, perpetually grinning, skeletal monstrosity.

Each exhalation from his nostrils was an eerie, metallic hiss.

The doctor reached inside his mahogany-colored, leather vest and withdrew an *El Ray Del Mundo* 'Piramides. cigar. He thrust the long, thick cigar between his yellowed teeth. The cigar ignited without the touch of a match.

His ghastly face, mahogany, leather three-piece tuxedo, brown, leather top hat, dark brown boots and worn leather gaiters gave him the appearance of a militant Baron Samedi – the Haitian Vodoun spirit of the grave. A fitting image for the Scythe of Death.

A flash of red and white whizzed by the hearse.

The Scythe whipped the hearse onto Peachtree Street and then he took off behind the speeding truck.

He slammed the heel of his combat boot down onto the accelerator as his gloved hand shifted the hearse into high gear.

The vehicle flew down Peachtree Street like a bullet fired from a carbine, quickly closing on the Coca-Cola truck.

The Scythe cut the wheel hard as the hearse came upon the truck's left flank.

The hearse slammed into the side of the truck.

The truck swerved to the right, squealing as its driver tried to right the vehicle.

The Scythe slammed the hearse into the truck's flank once more.

The smell of burnt rubber filled the air as the truck's brakes and wheels struggled against the hearse's onslaught.

The truck came to a crashing halt, its right side bending around the thick trunk of an old oak tree.

The Scythe parked the hearse a few feet behind the truck and then hopped out onto the dark street.

He vanished in a putrid cloud of dirt and then appeared a moment later at the driver's side door of the Coca-Cola truck. He dug his fingers into the door and then ripped it off its frame.

With a snap of the Scythe's wiry arms, the door somersaulted through the air, crashing to the ground several yards away.

The Scythe reached into the truck, wrapping his leather-covered fingers around the dazed driver's neck.

"No, please," the driver cried.

The Scythe yanked the driver out of the truck and tossed him onto the pavement.

He waved his hand across the driver's face.

The driver went pale. He thrust his palms before and above him, as if he was trying to escape from an invisible box. "No! Let me out of here! The walls...closing in...can't breathe...can't..."

The man fell onto his back, pursing his lips and sucking in air as if he was sipping it through a straw.

The Scythe stepped around to the back of the truck. He studied the large padlock that secured the sliding door. With one stomp, the lock snapped and fell to the ground. He pushed the door upward and inspected its contents. Inside were forty wooden crates, all marked with the Coca-Cola logo.

He stacked three of the crates on top of each other and then carried them to the back of the hearse, where he loaded them in. He then withdrew a stick of dynamite from the hearse.

The Scythe touched dynamite's fuse to the tip of his cigar. The fuse ignited.

He tossed the explosive into the back of the Coca-Cola truck and then leapt into the hearse and drove off, his tires squealing.

He peered at his side mirror and watched the Coca-Cola truck erupt into a ball of fire.

A metallic laugh echoed down Peachtree Street as The Scythe sped away into the night.

"I want this Scythe palooka's noodle!"

Ernest Woodruff pounded his fist onto his redwood desk. "Find him; give him the Broderick and then bring his battered body to me so I can lay eyes on that hatchet man's mug before I bash it in!"

"No disrespect, but that won't be easy, boss," the driver, from the previous night's attack by the Scythe, said.

"What?" Woodruff spat.

"Like I said, no disrespect meant, Mr. Woodruff," the driver said, his blistered face leaking pus onto the collar of his brown uniform shirt. "But the Scythe...he ain't no ordinary lug. The way he moves...the things he can do...it's like he's magic or somethin'."

"Magic, huh?" Ernest Woodruff said. "Well, if he *is* magic, he will be brought down by the best magician money can buy."

"Harry Houdini?" The driver asked.

"No, Houdini is an escape artist...a prestidigitator," Woodruff replied. "I'm talking about *real* magic...and a real magician...Dai Vernon."

###

September 6, 1922

Dr. Jerry Cygnet stepped into the lobby of his practice. Marie rushed to him, wrapped her arms around his neck and then planted a soft kiss on his cheek.

"Someone is in a good mood," Dr. Cygnet said.

"When I got here, I found not *one* crate of Coca-Cola at our door, but *three*!" Marie said. "Ain't that the bee's knees?!"

"It certainly is," Dr. Cygnet replied. "How did this minor miracle happen?"

"I don't know," Marie said. "I'm just grateful that..."

The door flew open, interrupting them.

Two men entered – one, dressed in a tailored, navy-blue silk suit and a navy blue Hamburg hat; the other, dressed in a brown Coca-Cola uniform jumpsuit. Pus dripped from his chin, soiling his collar. The man in the suit closed the door gently and then they approached Marie and the doctor.

Doctor Cygnet recognized the man in uniform as the driver of the Coca-Cola truck he attacked the previous night. The other man, he had never seen before.

"How can we help you, gentlemen?" Dr. Cygnet asked.

"The shine...umm...*shoe*shine man who works in the lobby of our place of employment told us the pharmacist here sells an over-the-counter salve that works wonders on burns and for pain," the man in the suit replied. "As you can see, my friend here is in need."

"Well, then, follow me," Marie said, walking toward her section of the practice.

The men followed closely behind Marie, admiring her curvy body as she glided behind her glass display case.

Inside the case were several bottles of medicine, jars of salve and bottles of Coca-Cola.

"I see you work for Coca-Cola," Marie said, nodding toward the driver's shirt.

"Yes, I do," the driver said. "We both do. My name's Mr. Wallace and this here's Mr. Wilson.

"Pleased to meet you both," Marie said. "I'm Marie; Marie Lefleur. Thank Mr. Woodruff for me, won't you?"

"Thank him for what?" Mr. Wilson asked.

"For the two extra crates of Coca-Cola that was shipped to me," Marie answered. "I figure the company did it to make up for the late shipment. Nice touch."

Mr. Wallace and Mr. Wilson exchanged quick glances.

"Well, here you go," Marie said, placing a jar of white cream on top of the display case. "That'll be an ace and a half."

Mr. Wilson slid two crisp one dollar notes across the counter toward Marie and then picked up the jar of salve. "Keep the change."

Marie plucked the notes from the counter and slipped it into the pocket of her frock.

The men turned and headed toward the door.

"See you around," Mr. Wallace said over his shoulder.

"You'd better hope not," Dr. Cygnet said, stepping out of the shadows in the lobby.

"What's that?" Mr. Wilson inquired, leering at Dr. Cygnet.

"If you see *us* again, that would mean you suffered some sort of trauma...some sort of calamity," Dr. Cygnet replied.

"I suppose so," Mr. Wilson said, opening the door. "Have a great day."

"You, too," Dr. Cygnet said.

The men left the office, allowing the door to slam behind them.

###

Marie removed her frock and tossed it onto the coat rack. She straightened her sequined, silver dress, running her hands along each smooth curve.

The door creaked open.

Marie snapped her head toward the door. "I'm sorry, we're closed."

Mr. Wilson – and two equally well-dressed men – sauntered into the office.

"Doctor Lefleur, right?" Mr. Wilson said. "These are my colleagues – Mr. Pratt and Mr. Turner.

"It's *Miss* Lefleur," Marie said. "I have a Doctorate degree in Pharmacy, so technically, yes; however, I am not a medical doctor and – not to be rude – but as I said before, we're closed for the evening, so if you'll please follow me…"

"What's the rush?" Wilson asked. "Got a hot date?"

"Actually, I *do*," Marie replied. "Now, please, go."

Mr. Pratt and Mr. Turner lurched forward and grabbed Marie's arms.

"We're going," Mr. Wilson said. "And you're coming with us."

"Let me go, damn it!" Marie screamed.

"Shut your mouth, smoke," Mr. Wilson spat. "Or I'll skin your black..."

"*The lady said let her go.*"

Wilson whirled around toward the metallic, hissing voice.

The Scythe stood in the doorway, the setting sun forming an eerie, silver-crimson aura around him.

"And if we don't?" Mr. Wilson asked.

"Then, I'll do this..." the Scythe whispered, vanishing in a cloud of dirt.

Half a heartbeat later, he appeared an inch from Mr. Pratt's back.

The Scythe wrapped his arms around Mr. Pratt's neck and then vanished with him. The air within the lobby was replaced with foul-smelling dirt, which left Marie, Mr. Wilson and Mr. Turner gagging and unable to see more than an inch in front of their faces.

Mr. Pratt's tortured screams tore through the putrid cloud.

Mr. Turner shuddered as the blood-curdling din crept up his spine and skittered into his ears.

Marie snatched her arm from Mr. Turner's grasp, dropped to her knees and – using her familiarity with the environment in lieu of her vision – crawled to her counter and took refuge behind it.

Mr. Wilson and Mr. Turner stumbled out of the office and onto Auburn Avenue, coughing the rank dirt out of their lungs and brushing it from their clothes.

The Scythe appeared before them.

"Where's Pratt?" Mr. Turner spat as he thrust his thick fingers into his suit jacket.

The Scythe exploded forward, driving his elbow into Mr. Turner's collarbone.

Mr. Turner screamed as his hand slid out of his jacket and fell to his side. His revolver hit the ground with a metallic thud as his arm bounced lifelessly against his thigh.

"That is a fractured clavicle," Lazarus said, pointing at the bulge in Mr. Turner's collar. "And this..."

The Scythe thrust the heel of his boot downward into Mr. Turner's knee.

A sickening crack – like the trunk of an old oak snapping under the force of a gale wind – followed.

Mr. Turner collapsed onto his back, screaming in agony.

"…is a torn lateral meniscus."

"You crazy son-of-a-bitch!" Wilson drew his revolver and squeezed the trigger.

The Scythe vanished just before the bullet met its mark.

He appeared before Wilson, thrusting his arm forward. The tips of his fingers speared Wilson's throat.

Wilson staggered backward, clutching at his crushed windpipe.

A burning sensation shot across the back of the Scythe's upper arm. He stared at it. A trail of blood spiraled down his forearm out of a thin gash in the flesh of his triceps.

He perused the area for his attacker.

A black Rolls Royce *Silver Ghost* limousine sat in the middle of the street.

A cabin door of the limousine opened. A man, dressed in a black, tailcoat tuxedo, exited the vehicle. In one hand, he held his top-hat, which he slowly slid onto his head. In the other hand, he held a deck of cards, which were spread like a fan.

The man drew a card and – with a flick of his wrist – hurled it at The Scythe.

The Scythe lunged sideways.

The card zipped past him, striking the door of the doctor's office. One corner of the card embedded itself deep into it.

He looked over his shoulder at the card – the tarot card of Death.

"Good evening, sir," the man said, bowing with a dramatic tip of his top-hat. "Please, allow me to introduce myself. I am Dai Vernon...magician extraordinaire."

The Scythe replied with a sweeping wave of his hand.

Mr. Wilson and Mr. Turner forgot their pain as they were ensnared in the crushing grip of fear.

Both men wailed in terror as they struggled to escape the stifling confines of some invisible grave.

Dai Vernon fell to his knees, his breathing shallow; his eyes wide with consternation.

The magician fumbled with his cards. With trembling fingers, he drew one from the deck. He licked the back of the card and then slapped it onto his forehead.

The Scythe peered at the card – an illustration of a broadsword with a golden crown hovering over it – the Ace of Swords.

The card's edges melted into Dai Vernon's forehead, becoming one with the tanned flesh. The sword and the crown oozed into the shape of a closed, vertical eye. The eye blinked several times and then opened wide. Vernon no longer appeared to be afraid.

The magician stood and – with rapid flicks of his wrist – unleashed a volley of tarot cards.

The cards sped toward the Scythe, whistling as they cut through the night air.

The Scythe disappeared in a cloud of dirt.

He reappeared before Dai Vernon and then lunged forward, driving the side of his head into the magician's nose.

Dai Vernon staggered backward, a web of blood spreading across his face.

The Scythe exploded forward, whipping his left leg in a wide arc. His shin slammed into Vernon's abdomen.

The magician flew backward, landing, with a thud, on the hood of the limousine. A trickle of blood fell from the corner of his mouth.

"That pain you feel is a ruptured liver," the Scythe said, appearing over the magician. He raised his fists above his head. "The pain you are *about* to feel is your face being pulverized into dust."

The Scythe brought his fists down with frightful force. His fists, however, met only the magician's tuxedo and top-hat, which Dai Vernon was no longer in.

The hood of the limousine collapsed under the force of the Scythe's blow. The front tires issued a loud popping sound and then hissed in protest as they fell flat.

He spun toward a rustling sound behind him.

Standing before him was Dai Vernon, now dressed in a white, double-breasted suit, white shoes and a white fedora. A red rose sat in his lapel.

Vernon held up his fists. Between each finger protruded a tarot card. The cards were fused with the flesh, forming rectangular claws.

The magician smiled and then sprang forward, slashing furiously with his 'tarot-claws'.

The Scythe parried and evaded the blows with feline grace.

One strike, however, met its mark, rending his glove and opening a deep gash in the back of his hand.

Another strike ripped open the flesh on his chest.

The Scythe grabbed Vernon's wrist and pulled him forward and off his feet.

Dai Vernon stumbled forward.

The Scythe hammered his fist into the middle of Vernon's forearm.

The magician's arm made a loud, snapping noise as it bent upward at an odd angle.

Dai Vernon shrieked in agony.

He twisted Vernon's wrist and forcefully pushed the magician's fist toward his own chin. He swiped the magician's claws across his own neck, slitting Dai Vernon's throat.

Blood sprayed from the wound in a wide arc and then rained down on the magician's suit, polka-dotting it with splotches of red.

The Scythe vanished in a cloud of dirt as Dai Vernon fell, lifeless, onto the pavement.

He appeared in the lobby of the doctor's office. "Ms. Lefleur?"

Marie rose from behind her counter, her fists raised below her chin. "Come on, then. Let's dance!"

"I mean you no harm, Ms. Lefleur," he said. "Don't you have somewhere to be?"

"Actually, I do," Marie replied. "But thanks to you, my dress is all covered in stinky dirt now, so..."

"Go home and change," The Scythe said. "I am sure he will still be waiting for you when you reach your destination."

"He?" Marie's eyes widened with shock. "How do you..."

"As dolled-up as you are...it has to be for a 'he'," The Scythe said. "Now, go; and don't fret, these men won't darken your door ever again."

Marie went to the door and peeked outside. "Dang, I guess they won't. Your handiwork?"

He nodded.

"Okay, then," Marie said, stepping out the door.

She poked her head back into the lobby. "Thanks."

"Go," the Scythe whispered.

Marie's head vanished from view. A moment later, the door slammed shut with a loud bang.

I gotta get that fixed, the Scythe thought, shaking his head.

And then he vanished in a cloud of dirt.

###

The Municipal Market was abuzz with eager shoppers of all ages and races.

While the white shoppers patronized the shops under the capacious tent that housed the market, Black people were only permitted to shop from the stalls lining the curb, thus to most Black people, the Municipal Market was known as the *Sweet Auburn Curb Market.*

While many complained about the racial segregation found at the Municipal Market and, indeed, throughout Atlanta, Jerry Cygnet welcomed it. The Sweet Auburn Curb Market reminded him of his beloved Greenwood Avenue and he believed that success and true freedom for Black people lay in owning and supporting Black businesses. And just as important was being able to defend those businesses – as the riot in Greenwood had taught him – with one's life, if necessary.

The Sweet Auburn Curb Market was home to a variety of shops, selling everything from the latest fashions to delicious pastries and confections. The Curb Market also boasted two popular restaurants – *Rolling Bones,* a makeshift shack constructed of tin that sold the best barbecued ribs and chicken in Atlanta; and the swanky *Sivad,* which featured a delicious menu from several islands in the Caribbean.

The owner, Milton Davis – a native of Columbus, Georgia – had traveled the world as the personal chef of famed historian, Carter G. Woodson. He picked up recipes and training tips everywhere he went, but the food he loved cooking and eating most was from Jamaica, Cuba, Haiti and Trinidad. Naturally, when he decided to open his own restaurant after relocating to Atlanta, Caribbean food would be his fare of choice.

Dr. Cygnet strolled past the booths, waving at the vendors.

"Hey, Doc," one called.

Good evening, Dr. Cygnet," another said.

He walked through the red, velvet curtains that hung over the doorway of *Sivad* and stepped into the restaurant's reception area.

The hostess, a beautiful woman sporting a black, sleeveless evening dress with a large, yellow, silk rose over her left breast, approached him.

"Hello, sir," she said, smiling. "Welcome to *Sivad*.'

"Hello," Dr. Cygnet replied.

"I'm your hostess, Lynnell," the woman said. "Will you be dining alone, this evening?"

"No," Dr. Cygnet answered. "I'm meeting someone. She should be..."

"Right behind you," a husky, contralto voice chimed in.

Dr. Cygnet peered over his right shoulder. Marie Lefleur stood behind him, flashing a bright smile.

Marie wore a sleeveless red dress with a hem that stopped just above her knees. The dress was embroidered with black beads in an overlapping v-shaped pattern that made her look as if she was covered in scales, like a snake. Her arms were covered in skin tight, red leather gloves that were studded by beads in the same pattern as her dress. Her hair, which was as black and shiny as her beaded pumps, was cut short and styled in curly finger-waves and a short necklace of red and black beads hung from her neck.

"You look stunning!" Dr. Cygnet, said, turning to face Marie.

"Why, thank you, Dr. Cygnet," Marie said.

She rubbed her fingers along the left sleeve of the doctor's navy blue, mohair, three-piece suit. "You're looking pretty keen yourself, Doc?"

"Thank you," Dr. Cygnet replied. "Lynnell, can you please show us to our table?"

"Certainly," Lynnell answered. "Right this way."

Lynnell sauntered toward a small, cherry oak table, with two matching cherry oak chairs, at the rear of the tent. Dr. Cygnet and Marie walked closely behind her.

"Here you go," Lynnell said, pointing toward the table.

"Thank you," Dr. Cygnet said, pulling out Marie's chair.

Marie sat and then Dr. Cygnet sat across from her.

"Your waiter will be with you momentarily," Lynnell said. "Enjoy your dinner."

She then turned and walked back to the reception area.

"So what's good?" Marie asked, sliding her gloves from her well-toned, arms as she perused the menu.

"You've never eaten here?" Dr. Cygnet responded.

"I'm a 'Nawlins' girl," Marie replied. "I love my gumbo, my crawfish étouffée, my jambalaya, red beans and rice, muffalettas and my po-boys. You can't find much Creole or Cajun food in Atlanta, so I usually eat in."

"Well, since you love your red beans and rice," Dr. Cygnet snickered. "I'd suggest the *diri kole ak pwa*, which is white rice with red kidney beans, glazed with a marinade as a sauce and topped off with red snapper, tomatoes and onions. It's a delicious Haitian dish."

"Haitian, huh?" Marie said. "My grandmamma was a slave in Haiti. She and my granddaddy escaped to Mexico when her owner moved to New Orleans."

"So, how did you end up being born in New Orleans?" Dr. Cygnet asked.

"Grandma came back to New Orleans when she was six months pregnant with my daddy," Marie said. "She came back to kill her old owner, Mr. Sardis, because she blamed him for the death of my granddaddy, who suffered from a terrible lung infection after a severe whipping from old Mr. Sardis. That infection took my granddaddy's life."

"Septicemia," Dr. Cygnet said, shaking his head.

"Yes," Marie replied. "Hearing the stories about how my grandmamma kept the sepsis at bay for years with a tea made from golden seal and turmeric is what led me to being a pharmacist."

"So, what happened to your grandmother?" Dr. Cygnet inquired.

"She killed Mr. Sardis," Marie answered. "Snuck into his house and poisoned his food. Then, she disappeared for a few years. Everybody assumes she went to Mexico, but she wouldn't speak on it. When my daddy was sixteen, Grandma resurfaced in New Orleans as a free woman, bearing the name Claudette Lefleur."

Dr. Cygnet studied Marie as she talked. She was beautiful, with a bubbly energy and bright smile that made her look even younger than her twenty-seven years of age.

"What?" Marie asked, blushing.

"Huh?" Dr. Cygnet shook his head and blinked his eyes to clear his head. He did not realize he was staring. He decided now would be the time to express his feelings, since it was obvious he found Marie attractive.

"I like you Marie," Dr. Cygnet said. "A *lot.*

"I'm adorable, huh?" Marie giggled.

"And silly," Dr. Cygnet replied. "But that is one of the many qualities I like...I love about you..."

Marie gazed into Dr. Cygnet's eyes. "Love?"

"Yes," Dr. Cygnet answered. "I would like to..."

"We're hungry," someone snarled. *"And what we're cravin' ain't on the menu!"*

"Applesauce!" Marie sighed.

Dr. Cygnet looked toward the doorway. Three men, all dressed in grey, pin-striped, two-piece suits, stood in the reception area.

The largest of the three men locked eyes with Dr. Cygnet. He tapped his partners on their shoulders and pointed a sausage-like finger toward Marie.

"Hey, little girl!" The big man bellowed. "Come here!"

The man's teeth we're abnormally large. The canines jutted from his mouth, ending in wicked points.

Marie looked around nervously. "Me? He can't mean me!"

Dr. Cygnet placed his hand on top of Marie's to calm her. "Don't move. And don't worry; I won't let them harm you."

As the trio drew closer, Dr. Cygnet noticed that their skin was pallid; their black eyes, sunken and reflecting no light.

Customers and Sivad staff scrambled and scurried past the velvet curtains and onto Auburn Avenue.

"I am Leroy Lotus," the big, well-dressed giant boomed. "And these are my brothers, Luray and Larry. We don't wan't to hurt you, little lady. The Big Cheese just wants a word."

Dr. Cygnet rose from his chair. "Stay away from her!"

Leroy sauntered toward Dr. Cygnet. "Don't take any wooden nickels, sap. I'll rip out your..."

Leroy paused and sniffed the air. He craned his head forward, bringing his nose an inch from the top of Dr. Cygnet's head. He sniffed again.

Leroy tilted his head toward his right shoulder and squinted. "Father?"

Dr. Cygnet had no clue what Leroy was talking about, but he was not going to let the opportunity caused by the big creature's confusion slip by. He slapped Leroy across the cheek with his right hand.

Leroy slammed his ham-sized fist into Dr. Cygnet's chest.

Dr. Cygnet flew over the table from the force of Leroy's strike, rolling, head over heels until he crashed into a row of stacked, hardwood chairs, which fell on him, hiding the doctor from view. He had planned to be hit, which would give him the opportunity to fall, crawl out of view and then become The Scythe. He had not planned to be hit so hard, though.

What kind of creature are *those things?* He pondered.

"Doc!" Marie yelled.

"You killed father," Luray said. "The Council will not be pleased.

"He's *not* dead," Leroy said.

"He smells dead," Larry said, sniffing the air around him. "The Council…"

"The Council will not do anything!" Leroy hissed. "Because Father was never here, understand? He is not dead!"

Marie rose from her chair and stood defiantly before the brothers. "He'd better not be, leech!"

"So, you know who we are little girl," Leroy chuckled. "Good. Then, you know what we will do to you after our employer is done with you."

Marie slipped her gloves back on. She raised her fists to her chin and bent her knees deeply. "I'm not going with you to meet anyone. You, on the other hand are going to meet your maker."

Larry exploded forward with inhuman speed. He wrapped his long, thick fingers around her neck, nearly encircling it. "Oddly enough, we just did."

"You mean, you just *died*," Marie croaked.

Marie thrust the fingers of her right hand forward. A moist, cracking sound followed as the tips of her fingers speared Larry's chest.

Larry attempted to scream, but the sound was trapped beneath the gurgling in his throat. Brown gore spewed from his mouth. He staggered backward until his thighs crashed into a table a few feet behind him. He fell backwards onto the table, landing with a loud thud.

"Larry!" Leroy screamed. Brown tears ran down his cheek.

"Flapper witch!" Luray screamed, thrusting his heel into Marie's belly.

Marie grunted as the crushing force sent her flying. Her back slammed into the edge of the red oak bar and then she collapsed onto her knees, gasping for air.

"You'll pay for that with your un-life," the Scythe hissed.

Leroy and Luray whirled about toward the Scythe's metallic voice.

Nothing was there save a cloud of malodorous dirt.

The Scythe appeared behind the brothers. He wrapped his muscular left arm around Luray's throat and then vanished again, leaving Luray's body behind.

Luray's headless body slumped to the floor.

"No!" Leroy sobbed.

Leroy's eyes flitted about the tent nervously. He sniffed the air and then coughed as foul dirt rushed into his nostrils.

Leroy growled and then took off, sprinting out of the restaurant on all fours like a mad ape.

The Scythe appeared beside Marie. He placed the index and middle fingers of his right hand to her neck. Her pulse was strong.

The Scythe lifted Marie from the floor and hoisted her onto his shoulder.

He then vanished, leaving Sivad with foul dirt, dead vampires and many questions.

Questions that he, too, needed answered.

CHAPTER FOUR

September 7, 1922

Leroy Lotus sat at the other end of a long conference table from Ernest Woodruff. Woodruff's face was twisted into a scowl. He slammed his fist onto the tabletop.

"Tell me, Leroy," Woodruff spat. "Tell me how three vampires failed to bring in one little Negro girl. Tell me how you let The Scythe, who I wanted to question the girl about, slip between your fingers. I guess a dumb nigger is just as dumb in undeath!"

"Apologies for the failure with the assignment, Boss," Leroy said. "But, in all fairness, you can't do a thing when you don't know from nothing about it. All we knew was we were supposed to bring the girl."

"Fair enough," Woodruff said. "But the fact still remains that you failed to bring me the girl. What do you think I should do about that?"

"I think that losing my brothers is enough punishment," Leroy replied.

"I was going to allow you to hunt in my town," Woodruff said. "In the Negro areas only, of course. But now, I think it is best you take your black ass back to Savannah."

"I think old Leroy here could still prove valuable, father," a voice came from the doorway.

Woodruff looked toward the doorway. Standing there, dressed in a navy blue, double-breasted, wool suit was his eldest son, Robert.

"Robbie!" Ernest Woodruff said, smiling. "Come on in."

Robert sauntered into the room. He walked to his father, hugged him and gave him a kiss on the cheek.

"How's George?" Woodruff inquired about the youngest of his two sons.

"Still being a good boy," Robert replied. He's twenty-seven and hasn't killed a man yet."

"I don't think he has the stomach for it," Woodruff said. "He's more like his mother. So, what is this 'Leroy Lotus is still of value' business?"

"I can solve your Scythe problem," Robert said. "But, I need certain...connections. Connections Leroy has."

"Is that right, Leroy?" Woodruff inquired. "You have connections that I don't know about?"

"I suppose so, Boss," Leroy said, gazing at Robert side-eyed.

"Leroy, here is the nephew of the Vampire Overlord, Adelphon," Robert said. "Favored by him, too, I hear. He can get me a sit down with the Vampire Council. You know how persuasive I can be. With an *army* of vampires on our side, instead of four or five, we can eliminate the Scythe with ease."

"Why am I just hearing that Leroy is related to Adelphon?" Woodruff asked.

"We vampires know how to keep our secrets, Boss," Leroy said.

"Next, you'll be telling me Adelphon is a Negro," Woodruff chuckled.

"He is," Leroy said with a smirk.

Woodruff sat bolt upright. "What?"

"What?" Leroy snickered. "You thought a Negro as dark as I am had other than black blood in me?"

"Times are a-changing, father," Robert said.

"Obviously," Woodruff sighed. "And what about the girl? Leroy says she is as formidable as The Scythe."

"I had some friends of mine in the Bureau of Investigation look into Ms. Lefleur," Robert said. "It appears that Marie Lefleur is an alias. They believe that she is a Haitian spy and assassin known as 'La Vipère Noire' – *the Black Viper* – who is suspected of the murder of William Taylor this past February."

"William Desmond Taylor, the director and actor?" Woodruff asked, scratching his head. Why?"

"While he was in the Canadian Expeditionary Force, Taylor led some mission in Haiti on behalf of Canada and the States," Robert replied. "When he returned to Los Angeles, he was given the director spot on a number of big Hollywood films. I'm guessing it was pay off for a job well done. The Black Viper must have bumped off Taylor in retaliation."

"And what is her connection to the Scythe?" Woodruff asked.

"Nobody knows," Robert answered, shrugging. "Maybe they're partners; maybe he just stuck on the dame. When I find them – and I *will* find them – I'll get all the answers you need."

"And since you're my son and I taught you well," Woodruff said. "What do you want for your rendered services, Robbie?"

"I deliver the Scythe and the Black Viper to you and you make me President of the Coca-Cola Company," Robert replied.

"Bring me their heads and their hearts, on ice, and the Presidency is yours," Woodruff said.

"Consider it done, then," Robert said.

Robert hugged his father and then turned his attention to Leroy. "Come on, Leroy. I have a couple of white dames lined up for you to feed on. They're dolls, with some nice chassis, too."

Leroy grinned, showing his fangs.

"Yeah, I knew you'd like that," Robert chuckled. "Come on, boy, let's get spifflicated tonight. Tomorrow, we got work to do."

###

Hundreds of men huddled together.

The heat from the torches that encircled them warmed their shirtless bodies, calming the chattering din that crept from under the burlap masks that covered each man's head.

The night air reeked of sweat and cheap whiskey.

"Aliens!" A gritty, male's voice boomed. "Kigy!" – *"Klansmen, I greet you!"*

Hail the Imperial Wizard of Imperial Wizards," the men replied. "Hail Adelphon!"

A tall, powerfully built man sauntered into the circle of flames and stood before his brethren. His crimson silk robe clung to his muscles, pinned to him by the crisp wind that whistled across the forest. Adelphon's conical hood remained, somehow, steady, standing tall and defiant against the gale winds.

"Yeh stepped into this circle, this evenin', as mere men," Adelphon said, his Midwestern accent betrayed a hint of Scouse. "But tonight, yeh leave this circle as *more* than men. *Much* more."

As Adelphon sauntered around the men, his voice grew deeper, darker under his hood. "This evenin', yeh entered this circle as *Aliens*...as individual entities. Tonight, yeh leave this circle as *one*."

Adelphon thrust a gloved hand toward the black sky. "One is who we be; one people, one blood, one clan. And what be the name of this clan?"

"Kuklos!" The shirtless pledges shouted in unison.

"Who?" Adelphon inquired.

"Kuklos!" The men repeated.

"Who?"

"Kuklos!"

"*That's* who we be!" Adelphon shouted. "The Kuklos Klan...Brotherhood of the Sacred Circle; Saviours of the White Race against the pilferin', swindlin' masses of Jews; the savage, rapin' hordes of niggers; and the wicked manipulations of the Pope of Rome and his white-collared lackeys!"

"Hail Adelphon!" The men shouted.

"Hail the Kuklos Klan!" Adelphon replied. "Let the letters K-K-K be etched into all the annals of the histories of man.

Adelphon raised his left arm before him and saluted the men with his palm. "No Kikes! No Koons! No Katholics!"

The men extended their left palm toward Adelphon. "No Kikes! No Koons! No Katholics!"

"Let K-K-K be carved into the hearts of the enemies of the *true* Americans," Adelphon said. "The Kuklos Klan! Kigy!"

Adelphon turned on his heels and sauntered off, disappearing into the shadows beyond the light of the flames as the chanting of his name echoed across the cold, night sky.

Loudest among the chanters was Robert Woodruff, who wiped tears from his eyes as he extolled his master's name.

###

Dr. Cygnet sat on the edge of his bed, watching over Marie, who slept, wrapped in a wool blanket.

He closed his eyes and focused his mind on the darkness. He felt a tug in his back, then a pull. He felt himself drawn into a moist, mugginess.

The doctor opened his eyes. He was surrounded by blackness. Ikukulu flitted around his head, glowing brightly.

"I was wondering when you would come," Ikukulu chimed.

"Who is Father?" Dr. Cygnet said. His voice was cold.

"You sound upset," Ikukulu said.

"Being attacked by vampires is upsetting," Dr. Cygnet replied. "Who is Father?"

"I am," Ikukulu replied.

"Of those vampires? The Lotus Brothers?" Dr. Cygnet inquired.

"Of *all* vampires," Ikukulu answered.

"And you didn't think that I should be made aware of that fact?"

"I didn't plan for you to encounter them so soon?"

"Plan?" Dr. Cygnet spat. "So soon?"

"It is a long story," Ikukulu said. "And better to *show* you, than tell you."

CHAPTER FIVE

616 B.C.E.

Dr. Cygnet found himself standing outside of a large mud-brick house.

He knew this house. It was *his* house; or, rather, Ikukulu's.

On the exterior walls of the house were painted elephants, ostriches, lions, apes and snakes. Carved into the dark brown iroko wood door was a depiction of spear and longbow-wielding warriors going into battle with lizard-like humanoids.

My family's history, Dr. Cygnet thought. *No...Ikukulu's...mine...our..."*

He inhaled deeply, allowing his mind to give way to Ikukulu's memories.

The doors flew open. A middle-aged woman, with skin the color of cast iron, burst through the doorway and knelt before him. "Baba, my father has transitioned."

"Uncle Sola was a great warrior," Ikukulu said, patting the woman's shoulder with his onyx-hued hand. "He is a worthy vessel for the Abo."

The woman looked up at him and smiled. "I am sure he will prove valuable in killing many Jugu, Baba."

"It is what the Abo do best, child," Ikukulu replied.

"You Abo do enjoy killing, don't you?"

"An Agu!" The woman cried, pointing over Ikukulu's shoulder as she scurried backward on her haunches.

"He is not here to harm you, child," Ikukulu said. "Go back inside and receive the Abo when he awakens. Say nothing of the Agu, though; we do not want to alarm my brother."

Ikukulu turned toward the source of the voice. Standing behind him was a tall, sinewy man dressed in a crimson leather vest and matching leather trousers that clung to his legs like a second skin. He wore iron bracers, greaves and an iron collar. His feet were covered in crimson boots.

Ikukulu inspected himself. He was similarly dressed, only his leather clothing was indigo in color and the armor around his forearms, crus and neck was constructed from orange coral.

"No one is supposed to see us meet, except on opposite sides of the battlefield, Anesusu," Ikukulu said.

"Time is of the essence," Anesusu said. "We don't have time for discretion. The Jugu are storming up the Egbado Corridor and will reach Oyo in less than a sennight."

"Alright, then, I'll head to Ijaye," Ikukulu said. "Have your army gather there and then march to the mouth of the Ogun River. We'll cut off the Jugu there."

"Alright, we will meet you there by dawn," Anesusu said. "Do your fellow Abo know you have succeeded in writing the sigil?"

"They know," Ikukulu replied. "They do not want to use it, though. Working with the Agu is an abomination to my kind."

"Yet, *you* work with us," Anesusu said.

"My role as the Abo of Death requires I think independent of my brethren," Ikukulu said. "When I realized that the activation of the sigil required both Abo and Agu blood I knew I would have to act alone. To do the unthinkable in order to save us all."

"Well, the Agu will honor your request for a truce after we have neutralized this Jugu menace," Anesusu said.

"To eliminate the Jugu and to broker peace between Abo and Agu is well worth the price I must pay for my insubordination," Ikukulu said. "I will see you soon, Anesusu."

"Soon," Anesusu replied.

Ikukulu clapped his hands together. The earth beneath him liquefied. Ikukulu sank into it, his head rapidly disappearing within the reddish-brown sludge.

A moment later, the mud returned to its original soft, but firm, clay-state.

A few minutes after that, Ikukulu arose in Ijaye, a small village of farmers and hunters. Ikukulu was fond of this quiet, simple village of quiet, simple people and he normally chose his hosts from among Ijaye's dead hunters.

Possession of the deceased by the Abo was an honor bestowed upon a family and was considered much better than the alternatives – a dying relative's body usurped by the Agu, which left the possessed person's spirit displaced and unable to make its transition; or consumed by the Jugu, who consumed the spirit right along with the flesh.

The world knew them by many names – Abo, Agu and Jugu; Orisa, Ajogun and Elenini; Angels, Devils and Demons – whatever, the name, their relationship is always the same: mortal and eternal enemies.

The supernal Abo and the infernal Agu, while much more powerful than the abysmal Jugu, were far outmatched in numbers and ferocity. And while the Abo and Agu were beings of spirit that relied on possessing man in order to interact with, and affect, the physical plane, the Jugu were creatures of flesh, from another physical plane separated from the earthly one by a gossamer veil, which was shredded and passed through by the Jugu when man was still young upon the earth.

The villagers rushed out of their homes to meet Ikukulu. They knelt before the Abo of Death and greeted him. "E kasaan, Baba!" – *"Good afternoon, father!"*

"E kasaan, omo mi," Ikukulu replied. "Dide." – *"Good afternoon, my children. Rise."*

The people of Ijaye hopped to their feet. Their Ijoye – or Chief – Bunkola, approached Ikukulu with a broad smile and open arms. Ikukulu embraced him.

"It is good to see you, Baba," Bunkola said. "But we have no dead here at this time."

"I am not here to carry away any dead, or to facilitate the mounting," Ikukulu replied. "In fact, I am here to prevent your deaths and any mounting of the living by the Agu."

"What?" Bunkola gasped. "The Agu are coming here? Have they forgotten that this land is under the protection of the mighty Abo?"

"They come by my invitation," Ikukulu said.

"I am sorry, Baba, I must have heard you incorrectly," Bunkola said, chuckling. "I thought you said you *invited* the Agu here."

"I did," Ikukulu replied.

Bunkola's smile faded.

"The Jugu are headed this way," Ikukulu said. "They will reach Ijaye by midday tomorrow and you know what they will leave in their wake."

"Cloth and calabashes," Bunkola sighed.

"That is all that will remain of the beautiful people of Ijaye," Ikukulu said. "I have enlisted the aid of the Agu. I need their blood, mixed with mine, to complete the sigil that will suck the Jugu back into their plane and seal them there forever. But first, I must safeguard you from possession by any Agu. Bring me two laying hens, a he-goat and a large calabash."

The villagers scrambled to retrieve all that Ikukulu requested. Within a quarter of an hour, two red laying hens, a big, white he-goat and a calabash gourd the circumference of half a mature pumpkin, laid before him.

Ikukulu drew his knife from its leather sheath. The brilliant sun glinted off the surface of the orange coral blade.

Ikukulu grabbed one of the hens and slit its throat. He held the hen's head over the calabash, allowing the bird's blood to flow into it.

He repeated the process with the second hen and with the he-goat until the calabash was filled to the rim with blood.

Ikukulu slid his thumb across the knife's blade. He extended his hand over the calabash, letting a few drops of his own ichor mix with the animal blood.

"Hurry," Ikukulu commanded. "Take the meat and cook it slowly. Eat well and then go home. Stay there until I and the Agu are gone."

Ikukulu picked up the calabash and then walked toward the houses in the village. At each house, he dipped his index and middle finger into the blood and then drew a sigil above the door – an octagon with an eye in the middle of it, at the center of which was a tiny 'x'.

By the time he had drawn the last sigil, the calabash was empty and the villagers' bellies were full.

"The sigils above your doors will keep an Agu from entering your home, as long as you keep your doors shut," Ikukulu said as the villagers approached their houses. "The Agu arrive at dawn. Remain indoors until we depart."

"As you command, Baba," Bunkola said, kneeling before Ikukulu.

The villagers, following their Ijoye, fell onto both knees and lowered their gazes.

"E kurole," Ikukulu said, turning on his heels – *"Good evening."*

"E kurole, Baba," the villagers responded in unison.

As he walked away, he heard the clicking din of bolts sliding into doorjambs.

Ikukulu turned his gaze upward. The sky was a beautiful lavender rose hue.

He clapped his hands together, liquefying the earth beneath his feet. Ikukulu vanished into the earth, rising a minute later at the Ogun River.

Ikukulu approached a massive, old kuka tree near the river's edge. He drew his knife and carved a large arch-shaped sigil into the tree's broad trunk. At the top of the arch, he carved a spiral and at the arch's base, he carved squiggly line. He then sat on his haunches at the base of the tree and pressed his back to its trunk.

Ikukulu closed his eyes and cleared his mind, allowing nothing but the image of the arch-shaped sigil to enter his thoughts.

"He who sleeps with an itching anus wakes up with smelly fingers."

Ikukulu opened his eyes. Anesusu stood over him smiling. A horde of Agu stood behind him.

"Only a madman would go to sleep with his roof on fire," Ikukulu replied, hopping to his feet.

"This is the sigil, then?" Anesusu inquired, pointing at the carving on the kuka tree.

Ikukulu nodded. "It is. It will require all of our blood to activate it."

"Let's get to it, then," Anesusu said, drawing his knife.

Anesusu held his obsidian blade high above his head.

Hundreds of similar obsidian knives, with gazelle antler handles, were thrust into the air.

Ikukulu drew his coral knife. He slid the blade across his palm, rending his flesh and then pressed the leaking gash to the sigil for a few moments.

Anesusu followed him and then each warrior from amongst the Agu did the same until the sigil was covered in gore.

"The sigil is now activated and well-fed," Anesusu said to his brethren. "The Jugu will be upon us in a few hours and we will send them to their doom. So drink; make love – preferably not with your own wife or husband, for you married warriors – and rest up...for at midday, we usher in a new era...a new world!"

A cheer erupted from the army of Agu.

Ikukulu turned away and sauntered toward the river. The ways of the Agu disgusted him, but the refusal of his own brothers and sisters to work with the Agu had forced him to ally with them alone – a dangerous undertaking, indeed, but one most necessary. He prayed that his punishment would not be too harsh and that the Abo would one day come to realize his level of sacrifice.

Ikukulu and Anesusu stood at the edge of the Ogun river with three hundred armored Agu behind them.

The dawn air was cool; crisp; and carried the scent of sulfur and putrid flesh.

"The Jugu are close," Ikukulu shouted, drawing his knife.

"Swords!" Anesusu commanded.

The Agu drew their knives and pointed them skyward. A white energy, like a bolt of lightning, coursed through the obsidian blades, from base to point. A moment later, the knives expanded into broadswords.

Ikukulu knelt, slamming the pommel of his knife into the soft earth. The knife twisted; shifted; stretched. Ikukulu stood, a razor sharp, coral scythe now gripped tightly between his fists.

A muddy, marsh- green mass thundered toward them.

Ikukulu charged toward the mass, his scythe, held low, cutting a swath in the red dirt behind him.

"Forward!" Anesusu ordered, pointing his sword toward the fast approaching mass.

The army of Agu followed their leader, keeping pace with his loping gait.

As Ikukulu came closer to the mass, the monstrous forms of the Jugu became clear. Their brawny, grey-green bodies stood upon seven foot tall frames and their thick skin was scaled and ridged like that of a crocodile. Their facial features were human, but their mouths were extended, tapering into a 'v', like the maw of a crocodile.

The creatures roared in unison, exposing their dagger-like teeth. They raised their arms shoulder-high, baring their razor-sharp claws.

The Jugu had no one leading them, for their Mistress, Kielgek, commanded her warriors – with whom she was psychically linked – from the Abysmal Plane.

Ikukulu leapt into the fray, his scythe slashing furiously. The coral blade met scale-armored flesh and Jugu fell.

With each death of a Jugu, Kielgek cried out in agony upon her dark throne.

However, with each death of an Agu, of which there were many, she roared in ecstasy. Her warriors fighting on the Terrestrial Plane roared with her.

"Fall back!" Anesusu bellowed, turning on his heels.

The army of Agu about-faced and retreated from the battle, sprinting along the edge of the Ogun River.

Ikukulu whirled about and took off, running closely behind Anesusu.

Ikukulu could hear the Jugu galloping behind him, hot on his heels. He felt their foul breath on the back of his neck.

The Agu ran a few yards past the tree bearing the sigil and then turned to face their enemy.

Ikukulu dived forward, rolling past the tree.

The Jugu stampeded toward Ikukulu and the Agu.

Suddenly, as if the air had devoured them, the Jugu vanished.

Ikukulu turned toward the Agu. "The Jugu have been sucked back into their abhorrent world. You have done well, warriors! Now, quickly, we must fell the tree to seal the portal forever. Anesusu and I will beat back any Jugu who try to pass through until you bring the tree down."

"Work swiftly, my brothers and sisters!" Anesusu ordered.

Ikukulu stood a few feet in front of the tree. Anesusu stood beside him.

A vertical sliver of darkness rent the air. A scaly, grey-green head emerged from it, roaring.

Ikukulu severed the Jugu's head with an upward slash of his scythe.

Something slammed into Ikukulu's back with the force of a battering ram. He stumbled forward, his left arm, which held his scythe, disappearing into the black sliver. Something on the other side of the sliver grabbed a hold of him, piercing the skin of his forearm in several places.

"They have my arm," Ikukulu gasped. Cut it off, Anesusu!"

"I promised you that no harm would come to the Abo from the Agu, my friend," Anesusu said. "I must honor the truce."

"If you don't sever my arm, the Jugu will pull me into their world!" Ikukulu shouted.

"I keep my promises, Ikukulu," Anesusu replied. "I will not do you any harm."

A strong yank pulled Ikukulu's shoulder and half of his face into the darkness.

"You have betrayed me!" Ikukulu spat.

"To betray, you must first belong," Anesusu snickered. "You cannot run with the hare *and* hunt with the hounds. Goodbye, Ikukulu."

Ikukulu vanished from the Terrestrial World and the foul world of the Jugu welcomed him.

CHAPTER 6

September 7, 1922

"I was a captive for over two centuries in the realm of the Jugu," Ikukulu said. "For over two centuries, I was tortured and used to sate Kielgek's carnal appetites."

Why did Anesusu do that to you?" Dr. Cygnet asked, his thoughts, once again, his own.

"He made a deal with Kielgek," Ikukulu replied. "With the Spirit of Death no longer on the Terrestrial Plane, humans were immortal, thus, the Agu, who inhabited them, were also immortal. The Abo, with no deceased to inhabit, were quickly outnumbered and overpowered by

Agu. The few Abo with human hosts were forced into servitude, while the rest were unable to return to Earth and free their brethren.

"And you sired the first vampire with Kielgek?"

"Not in the way you imagine," Ikukulu answered. "Kielgek infected me. Not the body I inhabited; my very essence. My battered, weakened host body died. Spirit without flesh cannot exist on the Abysmal Plane, so my infected essence was expelled and returned to Earth at the spot of the sealed portal near the Ogun River."

"So, with the death of your physical form, you escaped," Dr. Cygnet said.

"Not exactly," Ikukulu replied. "Kielgek wanted me to escape. With my return to the Terrestrial Plane, the human hosts of the Agu suffered the ravages of two hundred years and died. And the Agu died along with them. All except Anesusu, who, per Kielgek's instructions, abandoned his human host the night before my return.

"So, he did not die?"

"No, but I did not learn of his continued existence until a thousand years later," Ikukulu said.

"And what did you do upon your return to Earth?" Dr. Cygnet inquired.

"I searched through the fields of the dead, ignoring the cries of the youth who yet lived and found the body of a young warrior who committed suicide after the death of his parents and wife, who was actually over a hundred years old," Ikukulu replied. "But the moment I and the young man were one, I was overcome with a swirling sickness in my gut. I stumbled to the Ogun River, praying that the cool water would provide some relief. It did not. I vomited in the river, infecting it...and all who drank from it; bathed in it."

"Damn," Dr. Cygnet gasped.

"Not damn," Ikukulu replied. "*Damned.* Within three days, every surviving villager in Ijaye had joined their once immortal relatives in death. But they did not stay dead. They rose – stronger and faster than a leopard and ravenous for human blood. In my weakened condition, I was unable to stop their migration from Ijaye and within a fortnight, vampires – called *Fanpaya* by the people of Oyo and Ile Ife – were preying upon men from Sierra Leone to as far east as Abyssinia and from Tripoli to as far south as Rhodesia."

"And the Abo were powerless to stop them?" Dr. Cygnet asked.

"They were too busy plotting my punishment," Ikukulu said. "For my insubordination and the resultant damage, I was stripped of my responsibilities as the Spirit of Death. I was forced to transfer that position and its powers to my son, Iku. My essence was then imprisoned in my scythe. I became the weapon I had used to kill scores of Agu and Jugu; the tool that my son used to reap souls."

"And now?"

"Now I hide from the Abo within your Ori," Ikukulu replied. "I will surrender to the Abo once my vampire progeny are no more and I have removed Anesusu's head from his shoulders."

"Is he a vampire, too?" Dr. Cygnet asked.

"He is their Lord and Master," Ikukulu said. "Anesusu inhabited a great warrior just before he died and when he rose from the grave, he was, of course, more powerful than the rest. He does not have their vulnerability to sunlight and his craving was not for human blood."

A chill slithered up Dr. Cygnet's spine. "What does he crave, then?"

"The flesh of vampires," Ikukulu said. "He intends to infect the world to ensure he has it in abundance."

"And Kielgek?" Dr. Cygnet inquired

"She is linked to the vampires as she is with the Jugu," Ikukulu answered. "The vampires are her eyes and ears on the Terrestrial Plane."

"Are there any more secrets you need to share?" Dr. Cygnet asked.

"None," Ikukulu replied. "You now know all."

"Then, we're done here," Dr. Cygnet said. "Let's go. We have a lot of killing to do!"

###

Dr. Cygnet opened his eyes. A chill ran through him and goose-bumps spotted his flesh.

Why am I so accepting of my lot? He wondered. *Ikukulu has deceived me; lying by omission. My thoughts are his; are his not mine?*

Marie stretched, raising her arms above her head. She sat bolt upright, her eyes as wide as dinner plates. "Doc? How did I get here?"

"I brought you here," Dr. Cygnet said. "This is my house."

"But how? I thought you were..." Marie paused, sniffing the air around her and then sniffing herself. "My dress; it smells like..."

"The grave. I know," Dr. Cygnet sighed. "Apologies."

Marie leapt out of the bed, pointing her finger at Dr. Cygnet. "*You're* the Scythe!"

She paced back and forth, her bare feet making a sound upon the hardwood floor like drums in the distance. "Makes sense. You could have clued me in, you know."

"Like you clued *me* in?" Dr. Cygnet asked, raising an eyebrow.

Marie lowered her gaze. "About that...I..."

"Father."

The crooning, gruff baritone voice sent chills racing up Dr. Cygnet's spine. He peered out the window and looked down toward the street. A score of vampires stood there, their eyes glowing yellow in the darkness; their skin – all varying shades of brown – blushing from recent consumption of blood; their lips curled up in smiles, exposing their fangs.

Standing a few paces ahead of them was Leroy Lotus and a well-dressed young, white man he did not recognize.

"Vampires," Dr. Cygnet whispered, snatching his mask from his chest-of-drawers. "An army of them."

"They know who I am," Marie whispered. "They have probably figured out who you are, too."

"Who *are* you, Marie?" Dr. Cygnet asked. "Hell, is your name even Marie?"

"I think, right now, we have more to worry about than my name," Marie replied. "Just know that, with you, I was *always* real; always *will* be."

"Father, we need to talk," Leroy Lotus shouted. "Are you coming out, or are we coming in?"

"I don't know much about your kind," Dr. Cygnet shouted out of the window. "But, I *do* know that you can only enter my home if I invite you."

"It's true that we vampires need an invitation," Leroy replied. "Silly vulnerabilities and all that; but Big Bertha need only knock; and she knocks *hard*."

"Big Bertha?" Dr. Cygnet replied, perusing the regiment of vampires. "Send her in and I'll send her back out with busted gams and a bad case of the heebie-jeebies!"

Leroy Lotus chuckled. The vampire army erupted into laughter.

"Oh, Bertha!" Leroy called.

A second later, a loud whirring din split the night sky.

A noise, like a wrecking ball slamming over and over into a brick wall, came from the side of Dr. Cygnet's house.

Marie stepped behind Dr. Cygnet and peered over his shoulder.

From around the corner marched a massive creature of tarnished steel. Its legs were as thick as tree trucks and were each driven by powerful turbine engines and its arms, also given life by diesel engines, ended in 7.92 millimeter MG-08 German heavy machine guns. Bertha's torso was a thick cylinder, upon which sat a fearsome 419mm howitzer. The barrel was seventeen inches in diameter and over seventy feet long. In the center of the torso, a red light blinked intermittently.

Big Bertha pointed its howitzer face and machine gun arms at Dr. Cygnet's bedroom window.

"Applesauce!" Marie gasped.

"Umm…I'll be right down," Dr. Cygnet croaked.

The doctor slipped on his mask. A moment later, the Scythe stood before Marie, puffing his cigar. "Stay here."

"Like hell, I will." Marie said, slipping on her shoes.

The Scythe shook his pallid head. A metallic sigh hissed from between his teeth. "Come on, then."

The Scythe sauntered down the stairs. Marie walked closely behind him.

He opened the door and he and Marie stepped out into the night.

"Hello, Scythe," Leroy said, smiling. "Or should I call you Dr. Cygnet?"

"No need to beat our gums," the Scythe replied. "Get to it, vampire."

"Scythe, it is, then," Leroy said. "Hello La...La..."

Leroy turned his gaze toward Robert Woodruff, who stood beside him. "What was it again, Mr. Woodruff?"

"La Vipère Noire," Robert replied.

"Man, you make that sound pretty," Leroy said.

Leroy returned his focus to the Scythe and Marie. "Hello, La Vipère Noire."

Leroy looked at Robert. "Did I say that right?"

"Yes, you did," Robert replied. "The accent was pretty good, too."

"Why, thank you," Leroy said. "I speak six languages...Nipponese; Arabic; Swahili; Greek; German...even a smidgen of Spanish and Latin, but never got around to learning French. Maybe, after my work is done here, I and the family will visit 'gay Paris'."

Leroy peered over his shoulder. "How about it, y'all?"

The vampires roared.

Leroy Lotus smiled at the Scythe. "Ernest Woodruff would like a word with you; with you, too, Black Viper."

"Then he is welcome to come here and see us," the Scythe replied.

"Now, you know Mr. Woodruff ain't coming down to Negro Town," Leroy said.

"It appears he already has," the Scythe said, nodding toward Robert.

"Oh, this here's Mr. Ernest Woodruff's oldest boy, Mr. Robert Woodruff," Leroy said. "He's here to make sure I keep it cordial and don't rip off *your* damned head like you did to my brother."

"No need to keep it civil, Leroy," the Scythe said. "Because *I* won't."

The Scythe shot a straight punch toward Robert Woodruff's face.

Robert caught the Scythe's fist just before it connected with his nose. He smiled.

The Scythe tried to retract his hand, but it was caught in Robert's crushing grip.

"Oh, did I forget to mention that Robert here is now the host of none other than the Lord of the Blood Kin?" Leroy snickered. "Well...introducing the Master of all who walk in Darkness...the Imperial Wizard of the Kuklos Klan...Adelphon!"

"Anesusu?" The Scythe inquired.

"It *is* you!" Adelphon replied, his eyes widening.

Marie, taking advantage of Adelphon's confusion, slammed a side-kick into the Vampire Lord's side.

Adelphon winced. His grip on the Scythe's fist loosened.

The Scythe snatched his fist free, pulled Marie to his chest and then vanished.

A moment later, they appeared in darkness.

"Dr. Cygnet?" Marie whispered. "I can't see."

Dim light split the darkness. The Scythe stood in front of his hearse, his tall, wiry frame illuminated by the vehicle's lanterns. Beyond the hearse was a vast blackness.

"Where *are* we?" Marie asked.

"On the other side of the veil," the Scythe answered.

"Heaven? Hell?"

"Not quite," the Scythe snickered. "Just know that you're safe here.

Marie nodded. "Not worried; just curious."

"We can't stay long, though," the Scythe said. "Anything past three or four terrestrial seconds here and you cease to exist over there....*or* here."

"We've been here over a minute!" Marie gasped.

"Time moves differently here," the Scythe replied, opening the hearse's front passenger door. "Five minutes here is a blink of an eye on the Terrestrial Plane."

"And how long can you stay here?" Marie asked, sliding into the hearse.

"A few hours, maybe," the Scythe said, sitting in the driver's seat. "Perhaps an eternity. I don't know and I don't intend to find out."

The Scythe slammed his foot down on the accelerator and the hearse sped off. A moment later, the hearse appeared on Auburn Avenue; a blur, as it rocketed past Dr. Cygnet's and Marie's practice.

Marie looked back at the clinic. "I'm going to miss it."

"I will, too," the Scythe replied. "But we've been exposed. We need a new place to hide."

"I think I can help with that," Marie said. Where are you going now?"

"To change the rules of this game," The Scythe answered.

"Stop by my house first," Marie said.

"To pick up your uniform and your bag of...goodies?" The Scythe asked.

"Umm...yeah," Marie replied.

"I did that right after I dropped you on the other side of the veil," the Scythe said. "It's all in the back."

"Well, ain't *you* the bee's knees!" Marie said.

"Yep," the Scythe said. "*And* the cat's meow."

###

The Scythe stormed into Ernest Woodruff's office suite.

La Vipère Noire burst into the room behind him. She was dressed in a matte black cat-suit, studded with tiny black beads. Her boots, gloves and even her derby were all similarly studded in a reptile scale pattern. A black bandana concealed her face from her cheeks to her chin. Her derby was pulled low over her forehead and tilted slightly to the left.

The two vampires sitting on post leapt from their seats.

"Viper, take the one on the left," the Scythe said.

"Got him," the Black Viper said sauntering toward the vampire.

She extended her right arm, revealing a small, tubular, metallic flashlight in her fist. She pressed a button on the flashlight and bright, white light washed over the vampire's face.

The creature laughed heartily. "Sunlight hurts vampires, dinge; not tungsten filament-light!"

The Black Viper whipped her left leg toward the vampire's head in a wide arc. As her leg passed through the light, the studs on her leg seemed to swallow it for a moment and then spit the light out with the intensity of two suns.

The vampire screamed in agony as his flesh blistered and charred.

The Viper's shin slammed into the vampire's neck, separating his head from his shoulders.

The vampire's body collapsed as his head bounced across his partner's feet.

"Damn," the Scythe said as the head rolled past him.

The surviving vampire leapt to the ceiling and then clung to it like a spider. He scurried toward the exit.

The Scythe vanished.

He reappeared right below the vampire and then thrust his right hand into the vampire's back.

The vampire wailed.

"That's your spine I'm holding," the Scythe hissed. "The first vertebrae of your lumbar spine, to be exact."

The Scythe slammed the vampire onto his face.

Brown blood sprayed across the black and white checkered floor tiles.

The Scythe yanked upward, ripping the vertebrae from the creature's back.

The vampire gasped and then released a weak moan.

"He's all yours, Viper," the Scythe said.

The Viper held her left forearm in front of her flashlight. She turned the flashlight on and the black studs intensified the light to a blinding brightness. The intensified light struck the vampire, setting it ablaze.

The vampire cried weakly as it convulsed.

A moment later all that remained of the creature was ashes.

The Scythe pushed the door to Ernest Woodruff's office open.

Ernest Woodruff sat at his desk, puffing on a sweet-smelling cigar.

"So, they succeeded in bringing you here," Woodruff said. "Impressive, but what was all the ruckus out there?"

"That was us killing your vampire goons," the Scythe replied.

"Very impressive," Woodruff said. "I would offer you a cigar, but I see you have your own. Maybe I should, though; that stogie of yours smells like ass."

"Your son didn't bring us here," the Scythe said. "We came of our own accord."

"Where *is* he, then?" Woodruff asked, leaning forward in his chair. "I swear, if you hurt him..."

"He, Leroy Lotus and an army of vampires are probably hunting for us right now," the Viper said.

"Then, you're here to kill me?" Woodruff sighed.

"Not just yet," the Scythe replied.

"Why, then?" Woodruff asked.

"We have bigger fish to fry than you," the Scythe said. "I'm here to call a temporary truce."

"And you thought I'd agree to that, did you?" Woodruff snickered.

"You are going to agree to it and honor it," the Scythe replied.

"And why, in the hell, would I do that?" Woodruff asked.

"Because your son is a mule for Adelphon and you need us to free him," the Scythe answered.

Woodruff scratched his head. "Mule? What are you saying?"

"Adelphon is now more connected to your son than a fetus to its mother's womb," the Scythe said.

"Impossible!" Woodruff said. "Adelphon is a vampire. Vampires don't possess humans or anything else. You need to brush up on your supernatural lore."

"Adelphon is no normal vampire," the Scythe said. "He was once an Agu – what many call devils. He is not harmed by the sun; he feeds on the flesh of vampires and, while he can no longer possess a person by force, he can transfer his essence to anyone who invites him inside."

"Oh, my God," Woodruff sighed, slumping in his chair. "Robbie."

"We can save Robbie," the Scythe said. "If you honor the truce."

"How can you save him?" Woodruff asked.

"Viper, please explain," the Scythe said.

"Adelphon keeps himself supplied with his vampire food source through the secret society, the *Kuklos Klan*," the Black Viper said. "The Klan's outer circle, its public face, the *Ku Klux Klan*, is populated by racist white members of the middle – and lower – classes. Its inner circle – the Kuklos Klan – however, is comprised of vampires of all races and humans who desire to be turned into vampires. The vampires worship Adelphon as a god and consider it an honor to be consumed by him. They call it 'the joining'."

"And what, he craps them out as little vampire-gods, or something?"

"No, he craps them out as turds," the Viper replied. "If we cut off his food supply – meaning capturing and killing the members of the Kuklos Klan, we can weaken him and send him to a place where he *will* die."

"How many vampires are there in the Kuklos Klan?" Woodruff asked.

"Thousands," the Viper answered. "But, we just need to kill the local ones. He'll be too weak to travel; too weak to maintain possession of Robert. We'll return your boy to you, safe and somewhat sound."

"Somewhat?" Woodruff spat.

"The separation from Adelphon is going to have him a bit balled up," the Viper replied. "But I'm sure you'll find him the best shrinks money can buy."

"Okay," Woodruff croaked.

"What was that?" The Scythe asked.

"Okay," Woodruff replied. "I agree to the truce. But tell me something, you started this war...why? And why end it now?"

"You took something precious from me," the Scythe said. "And I'm not ending it; I just don't want to fight a war on two fronts and, like I said...Adelphon is a much bigger fish."

"Look," Woodruff said, pointing the end of his cigar toward the Scythe. "Whatever I took from you...I'll pay you what it's worth times a hundred; hell, times a *thousand*. Just bring my son back and let's end this for good."

"What you took from me is worth more than your damned money can buy, Ernest Woodruff," the Scythe hissed. "When this war with Adelphon is done, you're dead!"

The Scythe wrapped his arms around the Black Viper and vanished, leaving Woodruff retching from the stench of the putrid cloud of dirt that permeated the capacious room.

CHAPTER 7

September 8, 1922

The Scythe followed the Black Viper across the acres of grass at *Oakland Cemetery*, both moving, with feline grace, through the shadows.

The Viper stopped at a massive, marble monument – a sculpture of a great lion lying, mortally wounded, upon a stone. The lion hugged a Confederate battle flag to his chest and across the base of the monument was written *"Unknown Confederate Dead"*.

"The Lion of Atlanta," the Scythe whispered.

"Secretly commissioned in 1894 by Ayiti, through her front company, the

Atlanta Ladies Memorial Association," the Viper said, dropping her right palm upon the lion's nose.

The Scythe felt a rumbling beneath his feet. A moment later, the Base of the *Lion of Atlanta* slid forward and then to the left, revealing an iron ladder that descended into the shadows several feet below the surface of the earth.

The Viper climbed down the ladder.

When the Scythe heard the clomp of her boots strike something that sounded like stone far beneath him, he leapt into the hole. Two seconds later, the Scythe found himself standing upon a polished granite floor in an octagonal room with an archway carved into each side. The room was illuminated by a score of arc lamps.

The monument slid back into place, concealing the room below it.

"Welcome to our humble abode," the Viper said. "I have a few more around town, but I figured this would be more to your liking."

"And just *who* are you, again?" The Scythe inquired.

"Just a simple recovery agent for a simple nation," the Viper said.

"And a pharmacist," the Scythe said.

"That, too," the Viper said, smiling. "Come on; it's been a long night. I'll show you to our sleeping quarters and tomorrow, I'll give you the grand tour."

The Scythe nodded.

The Viper led him through the archway to his left. They stepped into a large room. The walls were covered, ceiling to floor, with white fleurs de lis on a royal blue background. A king-sized bed, with a broad, dark mahogany headboard and four mahogany posts – intricately accented with brass – sat in the center of the room.

The Viper leapt onto the bed, landing on her haunches.

A steel door slid down from the ceiling, sealing the archway.

The Scythe peered over his shoulder toward the archway. "Humph. Nice place you have here, Viper."

The Viper removed her mask, showing Marie's pretty face. She patted the bed with her palm. "Let's give The Black Viper and The Scythe a rest. Come, sit down, Dr. Cygnet."

Dr. Cygnet closed his eyes and took a deep breath. The mask shifted and hardened into its metal shape. It fell from his face, landing upon his extended palm. His dingy, brown, leather suit morphed into a pristine white dress shirt, hunter green bow tie and grey dress trousers. His boots morphed into furry, white bunny slippers.

Marie giggled. "Can you control what your costume transforms into?"

"Yes," Dr. Cygnet replied.

"That's darb, daddy-o!" Marie said.

Dr. Cygnet sat on the bed beside her. "Thanks."

"So," Marie said, scooting closer to Dr. Cygnet. "Cash or check?" – *"Kiss me now? Or later?"*

"Cash," Dr. Cygnet replied, pulling Marie into his arms. They kissed passionately, enjoying each other's warmth.

Dr. Cygnet pulled away from Marie, caressing her face with his fingertips.

"No more masks with each other," he said, gazing into her eyes. "Only truth."

"No more masks," Marie replied.

They fell into each other's arms and kissed again.

###

Dr. Cygnet awakened to the buttery, sweet smell of grits and fried shrimp.

He leapt out of bed. The granite floor was cool on the soles of his feet but his bare body was warm. He looked upward and warm air, which blew from vents in the ceiling, caressed his face.

Dr. Cygnet extended his right hand toward the Scythe's garments, which rested on a red oak coat rack in the corner of the room.

The clothes flew to him, wrapping around his muscular body and molding to him like new skin. He closed his eyes and inhaled. The clothing formed into a white t-shirt and white, knee-length shorts.

He opened his eyes and followed his nose. Those delicious smells were coming from the vents above him.

He approached the archway. The steel door slid upward, granting him passage.

Dr. Cygnet stepped back into the hall of archways. The smell of breakfast led him through an archway to his right flank. He stepped through the archway and entered a gallery with cream-colored walls and a blue Blabon linoleum floor. The cabinets, oven, stovetop and cold box were all pristine white.

In a corner of the room, Marie busily set the table with two plates, two glasses and silverware.

"Good morning," Dr. Cygnet said.

"Good morning, Doc," Marie replied.

Dr. Cygnet chuckled. "Even after last night, I am still 'Doc" or 'Dr. Cygnet'?"

"Even more so," Marie replied. "I do believe last night was the beginning of a beautiful relationship and I told you, I want everyone to know that my future husband is a doctor."

"*Was* a doctor," Dr. Cygnet sighed. "That part of me ended last night."

"After we bump off Adelphon and his army of leeches, we'll take our lives back," Marie said. "I promise you. Now, eat."

Dr. Cygnet sat in one of the two chairs at the table. The look and smell of the food before him – grits, scrambled eggs, fried shrimp and toast – was mouthwatering. He scooped up a piece of shrimp and some grits with his fork and slid it into his mouth. "Delicious. You are a great cook!"

"My mother taught me that a woman should be able to hold her own in every aspect of her life – cooking, hunting, mothering, making love, fighting..."

"Even spying and killing?" Dr. Cygnet inquired.

"If need be," Marie said.

Dr. Cygnet ate more of the food. He perused the room, noticing that he did not hear the familiar hum of compressors. "What is this place? Are the oven and cold box real?"

"Ah, you have noticed the silence," Marie said. "The knowledge of our scientists in Ayiti is far beyond what you might imagine. And this place is just one of several safe-houses throughout the United States that I have access to."

"Why are you here?" Dr. Cygnet asked.

"I came to the United States to retrieve a piece of the Ogun Wòch – the

Ogun Stone," Marie replied. "A precious ore that this government stole from my people."

"The Ogun Stone?"

"It is a mountain of translucent black metal. Its origin is unknown," Marie said. "The stone amplifies, a thousand-fold, any energy that touches, or flows through, it."

"The beads on your clothing…"

"All pieces of the Ogun Wòch."

"And America has this stone?" Dr. Cygnet asked.

"Not all of it," Marie said. "A baseball-sized chunk. However, if just a thousand grams of trinitrotoluene was placed in a container with a fingernail-sized piece of that stone and detonated, the magnified force would be enough to level three city blocks."

"Damn," Dr. Cygnet gasped.

"So, you see why the stone had to be retrieved," Marie said. "It was stolen by Hollywood actor and director, William Desmond Taylor – a military intelligence officer working on behalf of the United States and Canada – during the 1915 U.S.

invasion of Ayiti. I neutralized him after making him tell me where the stone was located. It was held here at Fort McPherson for testing. I retrieved it and then shipped the stone back home. The U.S. and Canada have been looking for me since, so traveling by air or sea is out of the question. I saw the advertisement you published in the *Atlanta Journal* for a Negro pharmacist to go into business with you and the rest is history."

"You know they'll just come for the Ogun Stone again," Dr. Cygnet said.

"That would be most unfortunate for them," Marie replied. "I hate violence, but I *am* ducky at it."

"That, you are," Dr. Cygnet said with a nod.

Marie sat opposite Dr. Cygnet and began to eat. "So, what's our next move?"

"Our?" Dr. Cygnet shook his head. "I appreciate all you have done for me, Marie, but I'm not looking for a sidekick."

"That's perfect, because I *am*," Marie replied. "And I think you'd make a great one."

"What?"

"Look, Doc', I am your partner – on several levels – now," Marie said. "So I've got your back. Like it, or not, if *you* go to war, I go with you!"

She pointed toward a Thompson submachine gun mounted on the wall above the sink. "Besides, I've been dying to try her out in the field."

Dr. Cygnet rubbed his chin. A bead of sweat slithered down his furrowed brow. "How good of a shot are you?"

"You don't hurt 'em if you don't hit 'em," Marie replied. "And I *always* hurt 'em."

The corners of Dr. Cygnet's mouth curled upward into a smile. "Then, I have a plan."

September 10, 1922

"Is she ready?" The Scythe asked, approaching the Black Viper, who stood before something large hidden beneath a canvas tarpaulin.

"She is," the Black Viper replied. "I present to you...Mahogany!"

The Viper snatched the tarpaulin off of the object, revealing what looked like a sleek motorcycle with a stretched frame and long front end with extended forks. The vehicle was covered in steel armored plating, dyed matte black. No wheels were visible.

"You forgot something," the Scythe said.

"What?" The Viper said, checking the vehicle like a mother inspecting her child before it goes outside to play in the winter snow.

"The wheels," the Scythe snickered.

"Oh," the Viper laughed. "This ain't any conventional iron, fella. Our engineers call it a *vole motosiklèt* – a flying motorcycle, or hovercraft."

"Let me guess," the Scythe said. "It flies on a magnetic field intensified by the Ogun Stone?"

"I *told* all the girls at the speakeasy you were a genius," the Viper replied. "Absolutely!"

"I am going to have to visit Haiti, really soon," the Scythe said.

"So, what did you name your hearse?" the Viper inquired as she tightened the straps that held her Thompson submachine gun and three ammunition drums.

"Name?"

"You *have* to name your vehicle," the Viper said. "It adds to your mystique."

"Then, I'll name it... *The Sarcophagus*," the Scythe said.

"Sar-*car*-phagus," the Viper giggled. "Clever."

"I try," the Scythe replied. "So, are we ready to fly?"

"Ready," the Viper said, tipping her derby.

"Then, I'll meet you just beyond the cemetery gates," the Scythe replied.

He vanished, but left behind no cloud of dirt.

"Thanks," the Viper said.

The Scythe reappeared. "For what?"

"For doing your disappearing act, but not leaving that funky cloud of dirt behind and futzing up my jalopy and leaving me a ragamuffin."

"I have been learning to control it...for you," the Scythe said.

"Well, don't I feel special," the Viper said coyly.

The Scythe shook his head. A moment later, he was gone again.

The Viper hopped on the hovercraft and pressed down on a steel pedal with her right foot. The vehicle hummed and then slowly rose off of its blocks. The Viper squeezed a lever on the craft's handlebars. The vehicle stopped its ascent and hovered in place. She pressed down on the left pedal with her left foot and the vehicle sped through the archway and into the hall of arches.

The ceiling opened above the Viper and she ascended into the cool, dark night.

The Sarcophagus and *Mahogany* raced, side-by-side, up Edgewood Avenue. Suddenly, the Sarcophagus disappeared, leaving behind a thick, billowing cloud of dirt. The Viper pressed down hard with her right foot and *Mahogany* quickly shot up into the sky, high above the pall of foul grunge.

The Scythe appeared in the midst of the cloud, standing between two houses.

As it dissipated, the Viper descended until she was beside her lover.

The Scythe pointed toward their practice, which sat on the next street over. Shadows moved within.

"They've camped out in there," the Scythe said. "I imagine they have also taken up residence in our homes."

"Waiting to throw us a blow, no doubt," the Viper said.

"Then, let's not be late to the party," the Scythe said. "I'll take care of the leeches; you find Big Bertha!"

The Scythe vanished.

The Viper rose into the sky, silently encircling the neighborhood.

The Scythe appeared in his practice.

Man-sized mechanical dolls strolled about. Wires ran from their backs, descending into the floor and into whatever powered them.

"A trap?" the Scythe whispered.

A rumbling din came from beneath him.

"Damn," the Scythe sighed.

The floor collapsed as Big Bertha's big gun burst through the floor.

The Scythe vanished, reappearing outside, across the street from his practice.

The building crumbled around the mechanical monstrosity. As it lumbered out onto the street.

"Applesauce!" The Viper spat as she witnessed the building collapse.

The dolls, which were attached to Big Bertha's torso, danced about like zombie ballerinas. After a short while, their dancing ceased and they rocketed into the air, dislodging from Big Bertha. Flames erupted from the soles of their feet as they flew higher and higher. Several hundred feet above the ground, the dolls burst in a colorful fireworks display.

The neighborhood remained silent.

The Scythe could only guess what the vampires had done to the residents.

A second later, he found out as hundreds of vampires poured out of the houses on Edgewood Avenue and the businesses on Auburn.

The vampires raced toward the Scythe.

"Kill him!" One creature shouted. "Kill Father!

"Father is too dangerous, Lord Adelphon says," another vampire hissed.

"Kill him and we live as gods upon the Earth!"

"He has fallen for our trap!" A third snickered.

The Scythe stood tall and defiant against the wave of death that rushed toward him. "If you bait a rattrap with cheese, be sure to leave room for the rat."

A swath of vampires collapsed, screaming in agony as fire erupted from every orifice.

The Scythe looked skyward. The Viper fired a volley of bullets, forged from Ogun Stone. As the bullets passed through the purple ultraviolet light emitted by her hovercraft's headlight, they glowed intensely.

As the bullets met vampire flesh, the ultraviolet light trapped within them, now as intense as the sun, burst free, reducing the vampires to smoldering ash within moments.

Vampires fell by the score.

Big Bertha aimed her machine gun arms at the Viper and unleashed a storm of searing lead.

The Viper veered diagonally downward to her left. Bullets whizzed past her ear.

She dived toward Big Bertha, weaving and ducking gunfire. She fired a burst of her own.

The Ogun Stone bullets perforated the automaton's torso.

Big Bertha staggered backward. A viscous amber liquid spewed from the holes. The diesel fuel rained down on the ground – and the vampires – below.

The red light in Big Bertha's torso blinked rapidly.

The Scythe vanished, reappearing a few inches above Big Bertha's right arm. He fell onto it, driving his fingers into the machine's steel limbs. And then, he vanished again. Big Bertha's arm vanished with him.

The automaton's red light flashed brightly. The metal monstrosity shook violently in an attempt to pull its arm from the Scythe's dark, otherworldly sanctuary.

The Scythe reappeared on Big Bertha's left arm. He vanished again, taking the thing's arm with him.

The Viper flew behind the robot howitzer.

The steel giant struggled to pry itself loose from its trap, to no avail. Thunder erupted from Big Bertha's big gun as it fired a round in frustration. Pieces of vampire flew into the air and then rained down upon the rooftops along Auburn Avenue.

The Viper circled Big Bertha's torso. She stopped, hovering before Big Bertha's light, which blinked erratically.

The Viper raised her 'Tommy Gun' and squeezed the trigger, firing a barrage of Ogun Stone bullets directly into the light.

A noise, like a boiling tea kettle, whistled out of the holes in Big Bertha's torso. Diesel fuel erupted from each hole in a *spray-spray-pause...spray-spray-pause* rhythm. Big Bertha's massive gun barrel slumped forward. The automaton's light flickered and then went dead.

The Viper swooped low, strafing the horde of vampires with her Tommy Gun.

Agonized screams rose from the horde. A score of vampires erupted into flames, igniting the diesel fuel on the flesh of their nearby kin. Fire spread throughout the crowd rapidly. The vampires fell into a panic, scrambling to-and-fro, spreading the fire wherever they went. Within seconds, two blocks along Auburn Avenue had become a balefire.

The Scythe appeared on Edgewood Avenue.

The Viper pulled up beside him.

"Well done," the Scythe said. "Adelphon should be good and angry now."

"Absolutely," the Viper said. "We burned his burgers."

The Scythe pointed at Big Bertha, whose massive frame loomed in the smoky distance. "And broke his grill."

The Viper laughed. "Now, what?"

"Now, we wait," the Scythe replied.

###

An hour passed and all was quiet.

For two blocks, Auburn Avenue was covered in ash. The air, though no longer blanketed by smoke, reeked of charred flesh and petroleum.

A white, Roamer Town Car came to a screeching halt before the wreckage that was once Dr. Cygnet's and Marie Lefleur's practice.

Leroy Lotus jumped out of the driver's seat. His dark skin and black, two-piece suit were in strong contrast to the alabaster vehicle. He straightened his red straight tie and the rose in his lapel and then sauntered to the cabin's door. He opened it and someone tall and lean slithered out.

"Adelphon?" The Viper whispered.

The Scythe nodded.

Adelphon was dressed in a ground-length, purple, silk robe and a purple, sharply pointed hat. Hanging from the hat, like a veil, was a full-faced purple silk mask with eyeholes. In his purple, gloved hands, he held two shiny, black obsidian broad swords with black gazelle antler handles.

"Looks like the trap failed," Leroy Lotus said. "I'll set my crew in motion; we'll find the Scythe and that Black Viper dame soon."

"No need," Adelphon replied. "He's here."

Leroy sniffed the air. "Where?"

The Scythe appeared several yards behind Leroy and Adelphon.

"Right here," the Scythe replied.

The Viper swooped down beside the Scythe. "Count me in, too," she said with a shrug.

Leroy whirled to face the Scythe. A wide grin was spread across his face. He ran his tongue across his fangs. "Adelphon *said* you Abo love killing. Damn, it looks like you *relish* it."

"I only relish my hot dogs," the Scythe quipped. "They go well with mustard, too."

"Oh, you're really funny," Leroy said dryly. "Ha, ha...you slay me."

"I'm about to," the Scythe replied.

"Well, let's get a wiggle on, then!" Leroy chuckled.

Leroy exploded forward, closing on the Scythe with blistering speed and terrifying ferocity. His fists were a blur as he threw a powerful combination toward the Scythe's face.

The Scythe raised his elbows to his brow as he bobbed and weaved.

The vampire's punches slammed into the Scythe's forearms and biceps.

The Scythe grunted as the muscles in his arms convulsed.

Leroy hammered his right fist into the Scythe's ribcage.

The Scythe collapsed onto his left knee. He extended his left palm toward the ground to prevent himself from falling onto his side. He then lifted himself into a handstand, shifting his hips to the right. Balancing himself on his left hand, the Scythe whipped his right shin into Leroy Lotus' left thigh.

A loud crack followed.

Leroy's thigh bent inward at a sickening angle. He screamed like a wounded dog as he staggered backward. He slumped onto his haunches, his face twisted in pain.

"That would be a fractured femur," the Scythe said.

Leroy rolled backward, popping up onto his feet in mid-roll. He patted his left leg and smiled. "And that would be my vampiric abilities healing that bum leg."

The Viper fired a barrage of bullets at Leroy Lotus' head.

Adelphon leapt in front of Leroy.

The bullets speared Adelphon's torso.

Adelphon gasped as he bent forward. His back coiled and his chin fell to his chest.

He looked up. His bright yellow eyes glowed beneath his hood.

The Scythe frowned and then blew a puff of cigar smoke into the air. "Humph."

Adelphon stood tall, expanding his chest and spreading his arms like a great condor unfurling its wings. The Ogun Stone bullets flew out from his torso and then sped toward the Scythe and the Viper.

The Scythe vanished in a cloud of dirt.

The Viper shot up high into the air.

The Scythe reappeared, launching a vicious salvo of bone-crushing punches and kicks at Adelphon's body and head.

Adelphon bobbed, weaved and blocked the strikes. He then countered with a slash of his swords in a figure-eight motion.

The Scythe disappeared, reappearing at Adelphon's right flank. He then slammed his right elbow into the side of Adelphon's head.

The pointed cone of Adelphon's hood collapsed, like a sugar cone slipping off of a fallen scoop of ice cream. The Vampire Lord staggered sideways.

The Scythe darted forward, thrusting a heel kick toward Adelphon's lower back.

Adelphon whirled about, thrusting the sword in his left hand forward.

The sword tore through the Scythe's belly.

The Scythe gasped. Spittle sprayed from between his clenched teeth. He thrust his hands out before him, clawing at Adelphon's left wrist. He dug his fingers into the flesh and then vanished,

Adelphon's arm, up to the shoulder, disappeared with the Scythe.

"Argh!" Adelphon wailed. "Pull me free, Leroy! Now!"

"Yes, Lord Adelphon!" Leroy Lotus wrapped his arms around Adelphon's waist. "On three…"

"Just do it, fool!"

Leroy pulled with all his might, but Adelphon did not budge.

The Viper aimed at the top of Leroy's head and pulled the trigger.

Leroy released Adelphon and leapt backward, evading the shot.

The Scythe reappeared a few feet in front of Adelphon. "Seems familiar? You left me in this same predicament over two thousand years ago."

"Ikukulu, please, forgive me," Adelphon cried. "My arm…the pain!"

"That would be your host's arm ceasing to exist," the Scythe said. "Life can't exist in my realm for long. For example…"

The Scythe slammed his palms against the sides of Adelphon's head and squeezed, trapping it between his hands and then he vanished.

The Scythe appeared in his dark realm with Adelphon's head. He released his vice-like grip on Adelphon's skull. The hooded head seemed to hover in space

"Welcome to my humble abode," the Scythe said, spreading his arms wide.

"No!" Adelphon, screamed.

"I promised Ernest Woodruff I'd return his son to him, but I didn't say he'd have a head on his shoulders," the Scythe said, snatching the hood off of Adelphon's head.

Staring at him, a wide-eyed expression of terror plastered to his face, was Ernest Woodruff.

"Humph," the Scythe grunted.

"Woodruff didn't trust yeh," Adelphon said. He came to me with his own deal; he offered himself to me in exchange for Robert's freedom. Possession of a man of influence like Woodruff would give me certain...advantages. I also now have the power to surrender to yeh; end yer war; grant yeh whatever yeh wish. Just let me go."

"Woodruff figured he'd kill two birds with one stone," the Scythe said. Save his son and use you to kill me. But it is I who's killing those two birds tonight."

"Ikukulu...Scythe...please!" Adelphon, bellowed.

"Adelphon...Anesusu...nope," the Scythe bellowed, mocking Adelphon. "You and Ernest Woodruff are finished."

The Scythe blew a tiny cloud of cigar smoke in Adelphon's face.

Adelphon's face fell slack and rubbery. His teeth rained from his mouth only to be swallowed by the darkness.

A metallic giggle rose from the Scythe's throat.

Adelphon's skull collapsed inward. His face folded in upon itself, growing smaller with each passing second until it was gone.

The Scythe vanished, reappearing on the Terrestrial Plane just as Adelphon's headless body fell to the ground with a dull thud.

The Scythe perused the street, his eyes darting from side to side. Leroy Lotus and the Roamer Town Car were nowhere in sight.

"Where is he?" The Viper asked.

The Viper swooped down beside him. "I'm sorry. Leroy got away. He jumped in his vehicle and drove off. I figured I'd better stay just in case Adelphon survived."

"We'll find him later," the Scythe said. "Right now, I need you to take me back to *The Crypt*."

The Scythe pressed his gloved hand over the gaping wound in his gut.

"The Crypt," the Viper said, nodding her head. "So that's what we're calling our lair, now?"

"Every lair should have a name," the Scythe said.

The Viper chuckled.

The Scythe collapsed onto both knees. The Viper leapt from her hovercraft and ran to him, pressing her torso against his face to steady him.

His vision blurred and then a veil of utter darkness and silence fell over him.

CHAPTER 9

September 11, 1922

A rumbling, clattering din jarred him out of unconsciousness. However, the Scythe was still in darkness.

The pain in his abdomen was gone, replaced by a maelstrom of nausea.

Since becoming one with Ikukulu darkness, to him, was as clear as day, but in this blackness, in this gloom, he could see nothing.

A metallic gasp escaped his lips.

"Ah, you're awake. Good!"

The voice sounded familiar, but over the rumble and clatter in his head, it was hard to discern who the owner of the voice was.

"Who's there?" The Scythe asked. "And where am I?"

"I know you're all balled up right now, daddy," the voice replied. "But we're going to clear things up for you, so don't fret."

The world tilted and began to rotate slowly. The volcano of sickness in the Scythe's gut threatened to erupt. "Viper? Marie?"

"Attaboy!" The Viper replied.

"And me," a gruff baritone voice chimed in.

"Leroy Lotus!" The Scythe hissed.

"He *is* the bee's knees, Viper" Leroy Lotus chuckled.

"*And* the cat's meow," the Viper replied. "And that's why we're giving you a chance to live, daddy-o."

The Scythe closed his eyes, giving in to the constant pull of his dark plane, but the whirling, tilting chaos behind his eyes shattered his focus and the pulling ceased.

The Scythe felt as if he was collapsing upward, or sideways. His sense of direction and his place in space utterly abandoned him.

"That helmet on your head was made especially for you," the Viper said. "Built by the finest scientists in Ayiti."

"Courtesy of Kielgek," Leroy said.

"That helmet, plus the little concoction I injected you with while you slept, is what's making you feel so...out of sorts," the Viper said. "So you can't pull your disappearing act before we make our offer."

"I don't negotiate with monsters," the Scythe said.

"Well ain't you the pot callin' the kettle black," Leroy replied.

"I wasn't referring to you," the Scythe said.

"Oh, don't be like that, lover," the Viper said. "What I do, I do for my people."

"What do you want from me?" The Scythe spat.

"We want you to open the portal to the realm of the Jugu," Leroy replied.

"Free my mother, Kielgek and my brethren."

"I can't," the Scythe said. "No one can."

"You have the power to open portals into planes," Leroy said. "To create new portals; to travel between worlds others don't even know exist."

"With the power of the Ogun Wòch, you can open a portal that reaches into the Jugu's realm," the Viper said. "All they need is a crack; a tiny tear."

"And what are you getting out of this deal, snake?" The Scythe asked.

"Kielgek has promised to leave Ayiti untouched when the Jugu turn this world into their playground," Marie said. "And she has promised to let you live. You can live in Ayiti with me, or serve her for eternity. She really doesn't care."

"And you believe that?" The Scythe grunted. "Kielgek is going to pick the flesh from your bones the first chance she gets! Leroy, you don't have to do this. Your master is destroyed, he..."

"My master?" Leroy spat, interrupting him. "I *am* the master! I am the first of my kind; born to Kielgek and her consort, the San Bushmen hero, Heitsi-Eibib. It is Adelphon who served me. You killing my brother was a test. I needed to know you had the power to kill Adelphon."

"Why?" The Scythe inquired.

"We needed the blood of an Agu for the Viper's venom she injected into you," Leroy answered.

"Why not just kill him yourself?" The Scythe asked.

"Like all of my kin, I am bound by certain rules," Leroy said. "You can walk in the sun, but kill your brethren? Uh-uh. Who the hell imposes this bushwa?"

"Probably the Devil," the Scythe replied. "After I send you to Hell, ask him."

"Tough talk for a bimbo who doesn't know if he's coming or going," Leroy snickered.

The Scythe pushed upward on the helmet. He winced as pain slithered up the back of his neck.

"That won't work, lover," the Viper said." The helmet can only be removed by unlocking it. And I hold the key. If you agree to open the portal, I will remove it."

The Scythe lowered his hands and then nodded.

"Attaboy!" The Viper replied.

The Scythe heard a click, followed by a whirring noise. A moment later, the helmet was lifted from his head.

"And don't even think about disappearing on us," the Black Viper said. "While the nausea will now cease, my venom will still keep you disoriented. You won't be able to stand without help. Open the portal and I'll give you the antidote."

The Scythe perused his surroundings. The ceiling, walls and floor of the capacious, oval room was polka dotted with pebble-sized pieces of the Ogun Stone.

He saw that he was on his knees. He tried to stand, but fell over onto his side.

"I'm sorry, Doc," the Viper said. "But I have to do whatever it takes to keep Ayiti safe. I have to keep *myself* safe, too, so I'm not touching you. Get up."

The Scythe fought the disorientation and dizziness and struggled to his knees. He inhaled deeply and reached out with his fingers, envisioning worlds he had never seen, or imagined, in the deep recesses of his mind:

The emotional plane; where consciousness goes after physical death. Except for his; Ikukulu had kidnapped the Scythe's consciousness for his own purposes before it got there.

The plane of dreams; a realm of strange creatures, said to shepherd our dreams and nightmares.

Even the sparsely populated planes of the Agu and the Abo opened to him.

Finally, he reached the sweltering, craggy and twisted world of the Jugu. The acrid, yellow atmosphere embraced him. The smell of sulfur chewed at his nostrils.

A vertical, yellow wound tore open in midair in the center of the room.

A massive, scaly, olive green arm, as thick around as a young oak, slithered out of it.

Leroy smiled. "Come forth, my brethren!"

"Applesauce," the Viper gasped.

The Scythe extended his arms, closed his eyes and focused on the pull of the dark realm of Ikukulu.

A vortex of miasmic dirt, which seemed to appear out of nowhere, engulfed the room. A moment later, the Scythe, the Viper and Leroy Lotus found themselves in a vast blackness.

The tip of the Scythe's cigar glowed in the darkness.

The massive green arm flapped wildly at Leroy's feet and then melted into nothingness.

"Where are we?" Leroy spat. "What have you done?"

"I couldn't run from the party, so I decided to bring the party here," the Scythe said.

"How?" The Viper gasped. "You weren't touching us!"

"Thank your precious Ogun Stone for that," the Scythe replied.

"Okay, that's a nice trick," Leroy said, yanking the Scythe onto his feet. "Now, let us out of here and open that por..."

Leroy gagged as if he had just swallowed a marble. He staggered backward, clutching at his throat. A sharp fang fell from his mouth and shattered at his feet.

"You said it," the Scythe said. "You are the offspring of Kielgek and some Bushman hero. Like Adelphon, you are a living being and nothing living can exist here."

The Viper fell to her knees. "Doc! Lover! I only did it to protect my people, but I love you. I wasn't going to let them hurt you."

"*You* hurt me," the Scythe replied. "More than any vampire, Jugu or corrupt business mogul ever could."

The Viper fell onto her chest. With trembling fingers, she reached into her sleeve and withdrew a needle and syringe. Within the syringe was a black liquid. She pushed it within a yard of the Scythe.

"In your femoral artery," she croaked.

The Viper's body liquefied and then evaporated into nothingness.

"Marie!" The Scythe wailed. "No!"

He caught movement in the corner of his eye. He snapped his head toward it. Leroy Lotus supported his rubbery frame on his elbows and was dragging himself toward the syringe.

The Scythe crawled toward the syringe, his body swaying from side to side as he fought to maintain his balance.

Leroy reached the syringe first. He arched his back, raising his torso high off the floor, like a snake poised to strike. He then snapped forward, propelling his forehead toward the syringe.

The Scythe stretched out his fingers, snatching the syringe toward him just before Leroy's head made contact with it. He stabbed the needle into his inner right thigh, piercing the large femoral artery.

Leroy's face slammed into the floor, the granite beneath his forehead shattered. Leroy's torso shook violently. He wailed as his body was reduced to a thick sludge.

A second later, there was no trace of him, save his black, two-piece suit.

The Scythe injected the antidote into his artery. He grunted as white-hot pain streaked up his leg. After a few moments, the pain and the disorientation faded.

The Scythe leapt to his feet. A second later, he vanished.

###

Dr. Cygnet sat on the bed in *the Crypt*, holding the white cotton sheet to his face and crying as he breathed in the sweet scent of Marie Lefleur.

He closed his eyes and focused on the tug.

A second later, the doctor was in darkness, sitting upon the hood of *the Sepulcher*.

A brilliant point of light danced in the darkness before him.

"When a living creature dies here, in this...darkness, does its spirit go to the emotional plane I caught a glimpse of?"

"Don't even think about it," Ikukulu replied. "Let her go!"

"Just answer the question," Dr. Cygnet hissed.

"Usually," Ikukulu said. "But since this plane is a bridge between all the planes, a spirit can become lost in one of the other realms. A lost spirit is what humans call a *ghost*. The terrestrial plane is also such a bridge, which is why many ghosts reside there."

"And do ghosts possess humans, too?"

"No," Ikukulu said. "If they *do* possess, they inhabit *things*...furniture; houses; machines..."

And on Auburn Avenue, the light in the center of Big Bertha's chest glowed brilliant red.

The End

La Vipère Noire and the Initiation at Pic la Selle

December 15, 1918

The Voisin triplane soared across the evening sky; a great gray heron, circling high above the towering alp, *Pic la Selle*.

Standing nearly two miles high, Pic la Selle was the pinnacle of all Haiti. It was said that Pic la Selle was once a paradise, lush and home to all manner of fauna until the coming of the Lougarou.

None could agree on what the Lougarou looked like, as most who encountered one didn't live to tell the tale. Some said the creatures looked like large wolves. Some said the Lougarou resembled skinless men and women. No one was sure of what the creature looked like but what they *were* sure of was that the creatures craved blood and had a particular fondness for the blood of small children.

Almost no one knew how the Lougarou came to inhabit the great mountain peak; *almost* no one. *Sect Rouge*, however, was well aware.

Secte Rouge – or Sect Wouj, as most Haitian's whispered of them in their native Creole – the *Red Sect*, was a secret society of sorcerers, soldiers, scientists and spies charged with the protection of their beloved *Ayiti* – Haiti – at all costs. The Sect was feared by most, as they spread terrifying tales of cannibalism, kidnapping and torture among the people to conceal their true purpose and to make outsiders even doubt their existence.

It was Secte Rouge's triplane, acquired from powerful associates in France, which flew over Pic la Selle.

Inside the cargo bay of the bomber plane sat a man and a woman. The man's massive muscles tensed under the skintight, crimson body suit, which covered all but his chocolate brown face. The bodysuit was studded with smooth black, semicircular stones. The woman was similarly dressed, except her bodysuit, which clung like a second skin to her athletic frame, was matte black and atop her head, she sported a black derby.

Standing before them, pacing back and forth, was a short, athletically built man who appeared to be in his early fifties. He was dressed in a bodysuit that was crimson on the right side and black on the left. Atop his head was the symbol of Secte Rouge – a maroon turban.

"We will circle Pic la Selle once more and then it is time," the short man said. "You will cut loose your parachutes three meters above the ground and drop down at the site. "Èske ou gen yon kouto, A Vipère Nwa?" – *"Do you have your knife, Black Viper?"*

"Wi, Kòmandan," the Black Viper answered in Creole. – *"Yes, Commander!"*

"E ou, Krapo Rouge? – *"And you, Red Toad?"*

"N'ap boule!" He exclaimed. "Good!" "It is all you are allowed to take into your initiation; your knives...your hearts and your wits. Should either of those fail you tonight, we will retrieve your bones in the morning."

The Commander pulled a lever on the wall and the double cargo door slid open. A strong cold wind rushed into the plane, sending a chill up the Viper's spine.

"Ouverture ou kòmanse...kounye a!" – *"Your initiation begins...now!"*

The Viper sprang from her seat and ran toward the cargo door. She snatched a parachute off of a hook on the wall beside the door and then leapt out into the cold night.

She was a blur, spreading her legs wide and extending her left arm as she slid one strap of the parachute over her right arm. She then slipped in her left arm and finally, weaved the torso strap through its buckle and then pulled it tight.

The bright yellow static line attached to the interior of the plane slithered out of the Viper's bag. A second later, it went taut, snatching the parachute free. An upward-rushing wind forced the balled up canopy parachute open and inflated it.

The dome-shaped parachute slowed the Viper's descent. She peered upward and saw the Red Toad floating several yards above her to her left. She pulled the toggle with her right hand and veered slightly to her right. She looked downward. A tiny green rectangle sat amidst a field of dark gray stone. *That's the drop zone*, she thought. She pulled the toggles, adjusting her direction of descent with the push of the strong wind currents, to keep herself directly above the green rectangle.

As the Black Viper floated lower toward the ground, the tiny rectangle grew larger until it was clear that it was a patch of grass fifty yards long and thirty yards wide by her estimation.

The Black Viper drew her knife from the sheath on her outer right forearm. Its black-as-pitch blade, carved from Ogun Stone, shimmered as it drank the light of the moon.

The Viper slashed across the left parachute strap, severing it. She felt a slight tug to her right.

She then took the knife into her left hand and slashed the right strap. The parachute floated upward and disappeared into the night sky.

The Viper stared down at the grass ten feet below her. She inhaled, relaxing her muscles just before she landed. She landed on her feet in a low crouch, her eyes darting back and forth, searching the shadows cast by the line of trees at the edge of the patch of grass.

The Red Toad landed beside her with a dull thud. "Good, all is quiet," he whispered.

"Too quiet," the Black Viper replied.

"It's too cold up here for insects," the Red Toad said. "And the Lougarou killed off all the wildlife, so it's just us and them up here."

"Do you believe the Lougarou really inhabit this place?" The Black Viper asked. "Or is that just something to frighten initiates?"

"Hell yes, I believe it!" The Red Toad answered. "And the Sect Wouj scientists are frightening enough. They don't need to fabricate any stories."

"I find the scientists and their contraptions quite fascinating," the Black Viper said. "It's the sorcerers who I find...unsettling."

"I'll take magic *any* day over science," the Red Toad said, shaking his head.

"Magic *is* science," the Black Viper replied. "It's simply science that we don't understand yet."

"Interesting concept," the Red Toad said. "Let's discuss it further after we get a fire going."

"If we start a fire, won't that alert the Lougarou to our whereabouts?"

"I certainly hope so," the Red Toad said.

"Eskize mwen?" The Black Viper replied, raising an eyebrow – *"Excuse me?"*

The Red Toad laughed. "I'd rather face the deadly Lougarou – something we can possibly kill – than face the deadlier, undying mountain cold."

"You have a point," the Black Viper said. "Alright, let's gather the wood together though; no splitting up."

"Agreed," the Red Toad said, rubbing his palms together. "Let's get a wiggle on then. It's getting dark."

They crept toward the tree line, listening and looking for any movement. After a few minutes, they reached the old mountain soursop trees. The Red Toad reached up and snatched a fruit from a high branch of the little tree. He offered the prickly, green fruit to the Black Viper. She shook her head. The Toad shrugged and began peeling the fruit. A swarm of plump, yellow-white maggots wriggled around within the flesh of the fruit.

"Bondye kèt!" The Red Toad exclaimed, hurling the fruit to the ground – *"Goddamn it!"*

The Red Toad drew his knife and

began hacking away at tree branches as if he wanted to kill the tree for bearing larva-infested fruit.

An hour passed and finally enough wood was gathered and stacked in a pyramid shape to make a sizeable fire.

The Viper stripped bark from the tree for kindling and placed it at the bottom of the pyramid. She then handed her knife to the Toad.

The Toad struck the two Ogun Stone knives together and bright red sparks rained from them. They landed on the kindling, which then began to smolder. A second later, a small flame erupted from the bark. The flame grew larger until it touched the branches stacked above it, igniting the wood. The flame spread rapidly and within a minute, they had a small bonfire.

"Now, that's a fire!" The Toad bellowed. He handed the Viper her knife. "All we need now are some marshmallows."

"A starch-coated ball of sugar and

animal fat?" The Viper said, turning up her nose. "No, thank you."

"That poupou you are talking about ain't what I mean," the Toad replied. "I'm talking about *real* marshmallows, made from the sap of the marshmallow plant, which is then mixed with nuts and honey. The old *Egyptian* recipe."

"What do you know of sweets from ancient Egypt?" The Viper chuckled.

"A lot more than you could ever imagine," the Toad replied.

A cackling sound echoed across the sky.

"What was that?" The Viper whispered, holding her knife before her.

"I don't know, but I'll go check it out." The Toad replied.

"Look at the sky," the Viper said, thrusting the point of her blade skyward. "It's black as pitch now. You won't be able to see a thing out there."

The Toad thrust his knife into the

fire. The Ogun Stone blade began to glow a reddish yellow as it consumed some of the fire's energy. He raised the knife above his head and it illuminated the ground around him. "Problem solved."

The Toad then sauntered toward the direction of the sound. After a short while, the light emanating from his knife was consumed in shadow.

Another cackle split the silence. This time, it was much closer.

A screamed followed the cackling. An agonized cry that the Black Viper recognized as the voice of The Red Toad.

"Bondye kèt!" She spat.

More cackles, clucks and a low-pitched din, like the sound of distant war drums, erupted from all around her.

She glimpsed movement out of the corner of her right eye. Something large was rapidly moving toward her. The Viper thrust her knife into the fire and then hurled the glowing blade toward the movement. The thud of her blade was met with a loud yelp. A moment later, a massive flaming bird rose from the line of trees, like a phoenix, rising from the ashes of its predecessor. The bird let loose a screech that sounded like a wounded cat scraping its claws on a chalkboard and then plummeted to the earth. It hit the ground with a thud and then bounced from side to side, its flaming wings shaking furiously. After a few seconds, the bird lay still.

Out of the darkness crept a score of large birds that, to the Viper looked like a flock of nightmarish turkeys. The firelight revealed that in lieu of beaks, several spike-like fangs protruded from the creatures' faces, forming a sardonic mockery of a bill. Their featherless heads were blood red in color, as were their long, thick legs. Their feathers were dark and those that covered their wings were stiff and looked as sharp as daggers.

The Lougarou! The Black Viper thought. "Stay back, or I will kill you all!"

"Djòl fè dèt, dèyè peye," one of the Lougarou said. Its voice was gruff and nasal. *"The mouth makes a debt, the ass pays back."*

"Chen ki jape pa mode," another creature cackled. *"The dog that barks does not bite."*

"Come on, then," the Viper spat, crouching low. "Bondye fe, san di; neg di, san fe." – *"God acts, not talks; people talk, not act."*

Gobbles, cackles and clucks erupted from the flock of Lougarou. The creatures bounded forward in unison.

The Viper charged forward to meet them.

A Lougarou leapt into the air, slashing with its stubby wings. One of the razor-sharp feathers met its mark, carving a deep gash in the Viper's cheek.

The Viper staggered sideways from the force of the blow. Blood poured from the wound and her face burned as her sweat dripped into the wound. She fought through the pain, launching a flurry of punches and kicks in all directions.

The powerful blows, enhanced ten-fold by the energy-increasing Ogun Stones, sent several Lougarou sliding backward on their backs toward the tree line.

The Viper struck a low-flying Lougarou's thick body with a hook punch.

Ichor spewed from the creature's mouth. The force of the blow sent the Lougarou somersaulted across the sky and into the bonfire. A screech rose from the flames.

A terrible pain shot up the back of the Viper's right leg. She looked down to see a Lougarou chewing at the tendon above her heel.

She dropped onto her right knee and then thrust her fingers into the Lougarou's back.

A gurgling noise escaped the monster's throat.

The Viper snatched her hand out of the Lougarou's body, tearing a jagged chasm in the thing's back. She tossed the creature's heart at its feet.

The Lougarou's lifeless body fell over onto its side. Oily, black blood ran out of its mouth and the hole in its back, forming a foul-smelling pool around the creature's corpse.

A Lougarou ripped at the Viper's side with its talons, shredding her bodysuit and rending her flesh.

She grunted and then collapsed onto her belly. She fought hard to get to her feet, but the Lougarou were on her, ripping, tearing and biting.

Darkness threatened to overtake her. She blinked rapidly, desperately trying to regain her focus so that she could fight until the spirit left her body.

A black blur pulled a Lougarou off of her back.

The Viper looked up to see a large, humanoid silhouette tear the Lougarou in half. A booming din exploded from the silhouette. A frightening roar that shook the mountainside.

The Lougarou flew away, cackling and screeching.

The silhouette bent down and the

Viper saw it clearly.

"Toad?" She croaked. How?"

The Red Toad squatted before the Viper. His bodysuit had been replaced by a black, wool, two-piece suit and black, wing-tipped shoes with white spats. Upon his head, he wore a black fedora with a white band.

"We have a lot to talk about, baby," the Toad replied. "We're gonna get you patched up and you'll be right as rain, but please, don't call me *Red Toad* anymore. I hate it. It sounds like a foot disease."

"What, then?" The Viper coughed.

The big man smiled, revealing a pair of sharp fangs. "Call me...Leroy Lotus."

The End

WHAT IS DIESELFUNK?

What is Dieselfunk, you ask?

Well, *The Scythe* is a Dieselfunk tale, but if you still need it broken down for ya', here goes:

Dieselfunk is a type of fiction, film and fashion that combines the style and mood of the period between World War I and the early 1950s with Afrofuturistic inspiration.

Dieselfunk tells the exciting untold stories of people of African descent during the Jazz Age.

Think the Harlem Renaissance meets Science Fiction...think Chalky White (from "Boardwalk Empire") doing battle with robots run amok in his territory...think Bessie Coleman; the Tuskegee Airmen; Marcus Garvey; the Tulsa Race Riots...*that* is Dieselfunk!

Mob bosses. Nazis. Flappers. Jazz. Bootleggers.

These are the stuff of the era of Diesel*punk* – a grittier sibling of *Steampunk*, and the artistic subgenre that gave birth to Diesel*funk*.

Dieselpunk is a sub-genre of Science Fiction and Fantasy that includes – but is not limited to, or bound by – the aesthetics, style and philosophies of film noir and pulp fiction.

Dieselpunk features retrofuturistic innovations, alternate history and elements of the occult.

Think the movies *Captain America: The First Avenger*, *Sin City*; *Hell Boy*; the *Indiana Jones* films and *The Mummy* (1999 – 2008) trilogy.

Dieselpunk is set during the Diesel Era – a period of time that begins at the end of World War I and continues until the early 1950s.

Dieselfunk explores the amazing achievements of Black people during this incredible era, which was, at once, filled with wonderment and joy as well as tremendous tragedy, blood and grime.

Dieselfunk Archetypes – typical characters from the Diesel Era that represent universal patterns of human nature – will be quite familiar to most of you, as they are found in the two-fisted tales of pulp fiction, the classic noir films and mystery stories and even Blaxploitation movies of the seventies. Some of the Dieselfunk Archetypes are:

AVENGER

When the police don't have the manpower to help; when the Hard-Boiled Detectives demand too much money or just don't give a damn... there are those who will stand up for the weak, the oppressed and the victimized, fighting crime and evil in all its forms.

The Avenger is a shadowy figure who strikes fear into the heart of the criminal community, hiding their true identity behind a mask, scarf, or wide brimmed hat pulled low to conceal their face.

An Avenger's motivation is rarely known. Many utilize strange inventions, chemical concoctions and / or psychic or occult powers to give themselves an advantage against their enemies.

AVIATOR

During the Diesel Era, airplanes were still a fairly new concept. Most people had never actually seen one. Many adventurers raised some money, built a plane and put on shows to exhibit their skills. Some raced their planes, while others did stunt shows such as the famous Barnstormers of the 1920's.

Industrialist Howard Hughes made much of his fortune in the burgeoning aviation industry.

These daring men, more at home in the wild blue yonder than on the ground, were always on the lookout for adventure and the opportunity to make a few bucks.

Others served in the war and proved themselves the Aces of the sky – modern-day knights, racing over the battlefield, delivering a hail of hell in the form of hot lead on the troops far below.

DOCTOR OF MEDICINE

The Doctor can be a general practitioner, surgeon or other specialist, a psychiatrist, or an independent medical researcher.

A doctor seeks to help patients, promote a more rational and health-conscious society and, of course, to acquire money and prestige.

The Psychiatrist is a Doctor of Medicine who diagnoses mental disorders and administers treatment for the same. He or she can also diagnose and treat medical conditions.

ENTERTAINER

This archetype includes dancers, singers, jugglers, stage magicians, athletes, musician, actors and anyone else who earns their living in front of an audience.

It is applause, accolades, artistic expression, glory and / or money that drives them.

EXPLORER

The explorer braves the unknown, searching for long buried treasure, ancient and arcane knowledge or what lies beyond, beneath, or between.

Whether searching the wonders high in the Tibetan Mountains, at the center of the Earth, or in the depths of the sea, the Explorer will always venture where none others dare tread.

FEMME FATALE / PLAYBOY

An irresistibly attractive man (*Playboy*) or woman (*Femme Fatale*) who uses his or her many charms to convince others to provide some good, service or favor.

They are the perfect foils for a trusting, heroic adventurer who is often unfamiliar with the wily ways of these men and women. They are dangerous and willing to use their beauty – or anything else – to attain their goals. While many use their powers of enchantment for evil, others use their charms to help others, or to bring about positive change.

These are usually anti-heroes who operate on both sides of law and order.

GREASE MONKEY

Grease Monkeys are the rough, tough and oh so ready mechanics, electricians and handymen / women of the civilian and military worlds.

Aces at repairing automotives, ships, aircrafts and appliances for the home or business, these men and women keep the world moving along.

HARD-BOILED DETECTIVE

With many police departments forced to cut back on manpower from dwindling revenue, many people in the Diesel Era turned to the private investigators for justice.

While in most cities, the "private eye" is licensed by the police and must be privately bonded as well, these gumshoes often work in the morally gray area between law and crime.

The private eye usually acts in non-police situations – gathering information and evidence for private clients in impending civil cases, tracking down fleeing or cheating spouses or business partners, or acting as agents for private defense attorneys in criminal cases.

A private eye has no problem separating his or her personal feelings from the job and will gladly work for the guilty and innocent alike, as long as his fee is paid. Of course, working on both sides of the fence is tough – the police see you as a civilian muscling in on their job, and civilians view you as a rent-a-cop without the badge.

A more sophisticated cousin of the Hard-Boiled Detective is the Consulting Detective, who relies more on astute, logical reasoning and a powerful intellect than the two-fisted gumshoe.

HUNTER

Whether they are stalking a lion across the Plains of the Serengeti in a rite to prove their worth as a man amongst their people, tracking down elephants for their

ivory, bringing a museum the corpse of a
Yeti for display, or riding shotgun on an
archaeological expedition, there will
always be a need for the Hunter –
explorers of unknown lands and seekers of
the next big challenge.

INVENTOR

Brilliant masters of gadgets and gizmos,
the Inventor is intrigued by the
complexities of technology and finding new
uses for metal, electricity and diesel
power.

The Inventor is an expert in advanced
mechanics and electronics, which allows
him or her to create devices well beyond
the normal capacities of the Diesel Era.

JOURNALIST

These men and women seek to uncover
and expose the troubles that plague the
world and to make the general public
aware of those troubles.

While some might believe that to be a good
journalist, you just need a notebook and a
nosy disposition, in reality, you must be
willing to put yourself in the thick of
things to get the scoop. You must be able
to skillfully use words to report and
comment upon current topics and events,

writing as many words in a *day* as an author may in a *week*.

Journalists work for newspapers, magazines and radio, often taking on the role of detective to bring timely and accurate news to the public. They are the eyes and ears of the city.

Constantly on the hunt for the next big story, Journalists will uncover the secrets that others need – and have a right – to know.

MAD SCIENTIST

The Mad Scientist blindly pursues knowledge and power. They gladly experiment on the living and dead alike, using brutal torture techniques to unlock the mysteries of the mind and brain and conducting breeding experiments in an effort to produce new species.

These devotees of Charles Darwin and Doctor Moreau fill their island sanctuaries with animal / human hybrids, clones of themselves and loved ones and strange conglomerations of flesh and metal.

MYSTIC

Trained in techniques from the indigenous people of Asia, Africa, or the Americas, the Mystic is an individual on a quest to discover the great secrets of the mind and body.

Through meditation, study and training, they have tapped into their psychic potential. Most mystics also have extensive knowledge of the martial arts from the culture their masters hail from. This gives them a distinct advantage during the Diesel Era, as martial arts are nearly unknown in the West during this period.

OCCULTIST

Occultists may be the wealthy widow, seeking supernatural truths from her deceased husband, or a champion of science, seeking to debunk the paranormal. They may be the college professor, student, or librarian who uncovers the sinister nature of the occult.

Whatever the vocation or preoccupation, the occultist dedicates him or herself to the study of the unexplained.

Closely related to the Occultist is the Parapsychologist – a scientist, interested in the observation of, experimentation with and measuring the power of the supernatural. Unlike the occultist, these men and women tend to be scientists, who hold degrees in physics, psychology, or medicine.

PROFESSOR

The Professor holds a Ph.D. in one or more areas of expertise and has earned tenure at some college or university. He or she is qualified to teach and has a reputation of excellence – or incompetence – in one or more field of study.

Professors often become involved in adventures as they search for such things as ancient civilizations, ancient artifacts, new technologies, or contact with extra-dimensional life.

SCOUNDREL

A scoundrel excels at making her way around the law. She knows how to be stealthy, break and enter, and cover her tracks. A scoundrel may be a street thug, con artist or even a daring and stylish cat burglar or a crime lord, who oversees a criminal empire.

SPY

Masters and Mistresses of manipulation, charm, deceit and infiltration, the Spy pursues a life of intrigue, politics and diplomacy throughout the world.

Most spies can ease their way into any group and have connections across the globe.

Similar to a Consulting Detective, his or her keen senses and insight into human motivations allow him or her to notice facts and behaviors that most others miss.

The Spy's weapon is information and thorough planning – they maintain numerous cover identities and always have a contingency plan and several escape routes, should a mission go to hell.

WARRIOR

The warrior is at the forefront of battle – whether on the side of justice and heroism or in the service of selfishness, wickedness or mad schemes to rule the world.

Warriors are skilled in the use of most modern weaponry, as well as basic hand-to-hand fighting techniques, tactics and strategies; many possess an expertise in a wide variety of weapons and are truly terrifying on the battlefield.

Warriors range from backwater pit fighters, to bold activists, to military sharpshooters and battle-scarred veterans of world war. They make a living at the only thing they are good at – fighting, killing and surviving.

As I continue to pen more Dieselfunk stories and as other authors contribute their stories to this subgenre – a subgenre begging to have many more stories told – it is my hope that you can always refer to this book and have fun pointing out the archetypes in the great tales to follow.

WHAT IS PULP FICTION?

Some of you are saying "If not the movie by Quentin Tarantino, then what in the hell is *Pulp*?"

Is it that nasty, fibrous stuff I hate in my orange juice, but my wife always buys, because – for some odd reason – she loves it?

What is Pulp?

Is it that early 80s British alternative rock band who sounded like a hybrid of David Bowie and The Human League?

What is Pulp?

Think adventure, exotic settings, femme fatales and non-stop action. Think larger-than-life heroes, such as Doc Savage, The Shadow, Marv, from *Sin City* and Indiana Jones.

The genre gets its name from the adventure fiction magazines of the 1930s and 1940s.

Pulp includes Horror, Science Fiction,

Fantasy, Mystery, Western, Fight Fiction and other genres, but what sets pulp apart are its aforementioned fast-pace, exotic locales, linear – but layered – plots, its two-fisted action....and those characters! As author Thaddeus Howze describes them: *"I like the larger than life heroes of the pulp era – loud, bombastic, often arrogant, sexy, outrageous and oh so violent..."*

The first pulps were published in the late 1800s and enjoyed a golden age in the 1930s and 1940s.

And – like most genre fiction of the day...and today – Black heroes were absent. Like most genre fiction of the day, if a Black person was found in pulp fiction at all, they were the noble savage...or just the savage.

However, in 1957, we saw our first Black pulp heroes with the duo of **Coffin Ed Johnson** and **Grave Digger Jones**, violent and vicious Harlem police officers, who operated more like private detectives, often going beyond police protocol to solve their cases.

A true master of the pulp aesthetic Chester Himes – an accomplished author and screenwriter before going to prison – discovered the work of popular pulp author Dashiell Hammett while serving eight years in an Ohio penitentiary for armed robbery. Himes vowed to write pulp books that would, in his words, *"tell it like it is."*

Upon his release from prison, Himes moved to Paris and – true to his word – wrote a string of what he called *"Harlem domestic detective stories"*, all but one written in French and later translated into English.

His first novel, *A Rage in Harlem* (1957) – first published in French as *La Reine des Pomme* and also known as *For Love of Imabelle* – which won the prestigious French literature award, Grand Prix de la Litterature Policière, gave us our first taste of the fearsome Coffin Ed Johnson and Grave Digger Jones.

Fans begged for more of these pulp bad boys and Himes delivered, with a total of seven more bestsellers and one unfinished novel that was published posthumously: *The Crazy Kill* (1959), *The Real Cool Killers* (1959), *All Shot Up* (1960), *The Big Gold Dream* (1960), *Cotton Comes to Harlem* (1965), *The Heat's On,* aka *Come Back, Charleston Blue* (1966), *Blind Man With A Pistol* (1969) and *Plan B* (1993).

While the duo frequently uses physical brutality, psychological torture and intimidation to solve their cases, Gravedigger and Coffin Ed have deep and genuine sympathy for the innocent victims of crime. They frequently intervene – even putting their own reputations and lives on the line – to protect Black people from the vicious and truly pointless brutality of the white, openly racist police officers in their precinct. Jones and Johnson generally go easy on – and even tolerate – numbers runners, madames, prostitutes, junkies and gamblers; but they are extremely hostile to violent criminals, drug dealers, con artists and pimps.

It can be said that Coffin Ed Johnson and Grave Digger Jones were the darkest heroes in pulp…and not because they're Black…well, that too.

The next Black hero in pulp did not come on the scene until 1983. Who was he? **Aubrey Knight**, a lightning quick mountain of muscle, trained to be a Null Boxer who fights in brutal matches while locked in a zero-gravity bubble.

Aubrey Knight is the protagonist of *Street Lethal* (1983), a jaw dropping pulp thrill ride, penned masterfully by veteran science fiction, fantasy and horror author, Steven Barnes. *Street Lethal* is set in a near-future dystopian Los Angeles in which Aubrey Knight must battle genetically engineered New Men, drug kingpins, brutal prison guards, a ruthless femme fatale and brainwashing similar to the horrific Ludovico Technique from the classic novel *A Clockwork Orange.*

Street Lethal spawned two sequels starring the street-fighter, null-boxer and virtual superman: *Gorgon Child* (1989) and *Firedance* (1993).

Barnes, an accomplished martial artist himself, gives us a pulp hero who is one part Luke Cage Noir and two parts Iron Fist...only cooler, savvier and more...well, street lethal.

A classic costumed pulp hero, the black-hooded **Damballa** steps out of the forests of Africa and onto the streets of 1930s Harlem to battle Nazi's bent on proving the superiority of the Aryan race.

Damballa (2011) is an incredible pulp adventure written by author Charles R. Saunders, the founder of the subgenre of Fantasy fiction called Sword and Soul and creator of the Fantasy icon *Imaro*.

The action does not stop as the titular hero uses his vast knowledge of Western science, African science and martial arts to expose and neutralize the Nazi threat.

Set in 1938, Damballa is a shining example of what Pulp is when it is at its very best: thrilling, visceral, tightly-plotted, well-written, fast-paced fun.

And the hero, Damballa, is a shining example of what a pulp hero in the hands of a master can be: a hero the reader can actually stand up and cheer for; a hero with qualities and with a story other authors do their damndest to echo in their own creative and original ways.

Equal parts James Bond, Indiana Jones, Doc Savage and The Saint, **Dillon** – by his creator Derrick Ferguson's account – first came to attention of the world a decade ago, when he began hiring himself out as a soldier of fortune. Dillon possesses remarkable talents and gifts that make him respected and even feared in a world of mercenaries, spies, adventurers, powerful technology and mystic artifacts.

Actually, Dillon first came to our attention in the Pulp fiction masterpiece, *Dillon and the Voice of Odin* (2003).

Dillon's actual age is unknown, but what is known is that he was born on the technologically advanced, doomed island of Usimi Dero. After the Destruction of his home, twelve year old Dillon and his mother fled to Shamballah, a monastery hidden in the Himalayas. Dillon was adopted by Shamballah's Warmasters of Liguria, who spent the next seven years training him in various martial arts and other physical and mental disciplines. After those seven years, Dillon elected to leave Shamballah and return to the world.

Once back in the world, Dillon wandered,

learning various skills that would help him in his chosen profession as an adventurer and seeking out those who destroyed his homeland.

This adventurer is the hero of four of his own books – the aforementioned *Dillon and the Voice of Odin*; *Dillon and the Legend of the Golden Bell* (2010); *Four Bullets for Dillon* (2011) and *Dillon and the Pirates of Xonira* (2012) – and appears in the anthology *Black Pulp* (2013).

First seen in the often hilarious and always exciting, *Taurus Moon: Relic Hunter* (2011) and now returning in the recently released, equally exciting sequel, *Taurus Moon: Magic and Mayhem* (2013), **Taurus Moon** is a complex Pulp hero who walks a complex world of mythic creatures and gangsters and even mythic gangsters and gangling creatures.

The morally conflicted hero, Taurus Moon, is often compared to another famed relic hunter, Indiana Jones. Unlike popular relic hunter Indiana Jones, however, the artifacts Taurus Moon hunts are not found in the deserts of Iskenderun Hatay, or in the tropical rainforests of Brazil. Taurus Moon's quests take him through the grittier parts of urbanized cities; settings where Indiana Jones would not dare to tread. Also, unlike Indiana Jones, Taurus Moon's clientele includes vampire crime bosses and other individuals of ill-repute.

Taurus Moon is straight up mercenary, motivated by money; yet he is imbued with nobility, which keeps him from being completely amoral.

If Indiana Jones and Blade had a clone created from both their DNA strains, with a dash of Thomas Edison and Henry Ford sprinkled in, that little GMO fella would be Taurus Moon.

Throughout Africa, storytelling has always been an intrinsic part of society, used to recall historical events, impart wisdom, debate and communicate messages from the divine.

Storytellers – called Djele, Sanusi, Babalawo, Iyanifa, Okomfo and other titles, depending on where, on the continent, you go – are revered and are usually also skilled in spiritual and healing practices as well.

Tales of powerful heroes, megalomaniacal villains, sorcerers, witches and fearsome creatures abound in African folklore, thus I was not surprised at my recent discovery – thanks to Paul Bishop, author and mastermind behind the *Fight Card* brand of Fight Fiction Pulp books – that Pulp magazines, created by, and about, African heroes were highly popular across the continent in the 1960s through the 1980s.

Sold under the brand names *African Film* and *Boom*, these magazines – called photo comics, or "look books" – were illustrated with stunning photographs instead of drawings, giving them the uniqueness, creative flair and do-it-yourself spirit common throughout Africa.

With heroes like the Tarzanesque **Fearless Fang** (Boom) and the "African Superman", **Son of Samson**, children and adults alike waited eagerly every month for latest edition to hit the newsstands.

The most popular photo comic magazine was *The Spear* (African Film), which featured **Lance Spearman**, the super-spy / detective whose coolness James Bond and Derek Flint would envy. The Spear drove a Corvette stingray, sported a panama hat and well-tailored suits with a bow tie and smoked expensive cigars. And in true Pulp fashion, he had a bevy of beautiful women at his beck-and-call.

Lance Spearman pursued the bad guys with zeal, outwitting their conspiracies, kicking much ass with his African martial arts and saving the day...all in one issue!

These popular Pulps – a portfolio of black and white photos, complete with speech balloons, narration boxes and all the "bam-pow" sound effects that a kick and a quick upper cut to the jaw makes in any comic book.

Unlike the popular Pulps of the Western world, however, which were rife with racist tropes of uncivilized, uneducated, spear-chucking cannibals, or damn-near naked noble savages, with objectified, ample body parts, Lance Spearman was sharp, stylish and sophisticated.

Even the jungle stalking Fearless Fang

was intelligent, witty, brave and well, cool.

Combining Western references with a distinctly African cultural identity, these amazing African Pulps presented a critique of colonialism and a significant variation in how the genre classically figured normality and otherness.

And they were entertaining as hell!

Published first by publisher Drum Publications in Nigeria in the early 1960s and later also published in Kenya and Ghana the photo comic had a powerful and lasting influence in fostering postcolonial pride and identity.

Its combination of extreme violence, melodrama, romance and glimpses of the glamorous life preceded and influenced the Blaxploitation craze in American cinema in the 1970s and its use of inventive DIY tactics to overcome budget constraints influenced the booming Nollywood film industry.

Other popular titles included *The Stranger*, about a two-gun toting, Black Lone Ranger-type hero; the romantic *Sadness and Joy*; and the serpentine shero, *Cobra*.

"Ok, you've told us *about* the photo comics, but how, and why, were they created?" You ask? "

Well, *Drum Publications* of Nairobi, Kenya – tired of the clichéd racist images of Black people in contrast to the heroic images of white soldiers and superheroes in Western comics – decided to create comic books that would appeal to Black men. They began photographing black men in adventures that were designed to appeal to the Black African population.

Drum would buy stories and then send the scripts to Swaziland, where a photographer would takes pictures of a cast of Black actors. They would then send the photographed strips to London, England, where the magazines were printed. Finally, the photo comic magazines would be distributed in West, East and South Africa.

The Lance Spearman title was the most popular publication, with circulation figures estimated at 100, 000 in West Africa, 45,000 in East Africa and 20,000 in South Africa. In fact, Lance Spearman had a greater circulation in Kenya than any of the local daily newspapers at that time.

The writers of these look-books were Black Africans, who were paid $65 – equivalent to approximately $508.00 today – for every script they produced.

Expected in the scripts were lots of fistfights and the bad guys always losing in the end.

The readership of these photo comics included men, women, boys and girls from small rural towns to sprawling urban cities; from the barely literate to highly educated professionals.

The man, who played the character of Lance Spearman, was Jore Mkwanazi, originally employed as a "houseboy" in Durban, South Africa, scrubbing the floors of an apartment for $35 a month and as a musician, playing the piano in a nightclub for $1.50 a night, when photographer Stanley N. Bunn discovered him and decided he had the tough, cynical, sophisticated face that was needed for The

Spear. In the role of the super-spy, Mkwanazi earned $215 a month.

Here is the original Drum Publications information, found in every issue of their photo comic magazines:

Drum Publications (E.A.) Ltd
P.O Box 43372
Nairobi
Kenya

Editor: J. Singh

Printed by
Printing and Packaging Corporation Ltd
P.O Box 30157,
Nairobi, Kenya

In 2014, in addition to this book you hold in your hands, I will publish *The Scythe II: Long Pig* and the sequel to my Sword and Soul novel, *Once Upon A Time In Afrika, Once Upon A Time In Afrika II*.

We're working hard to bring you the very best Pulp, Steamfunk and Dieselfunk, so stay tuned, Steamfunkateers!

Big fun is coming!

THE SCYTHE

ABOUT THE AUTHOR

Balogun is the author of the bestselling *Afrikan Martial Arts: Discovering the Warrior Within* and screenwriter / producer / director of the films, *A Single Link* and *Rite of Passage: Initiation.*

He is one of the leading authorities on *Steamfunk* – a philosophy or style of writing that combines the African and / or African American culture and approach to life with that of the steampunk philosophy and / or steampunk fiction – and writes about it, the craft of writing, Sword & Soul and Steampunk in general, at http://chroniclesofharriet.com/.

He is author of six novels – the Steamfunk bestseller, *MOSES: The Chronicles of Harriet Tubman (Books 1 & 2)*; the Urban Science Fiction saga, *Redeemer*; the Sword & Soul epic, *Once Upon A Time In Afrika*, two Fight Fiction, New Pulp novellas – *A Single Link* and *Fists of Afrika*; the Two-Fisted Dieselfunk Pulp, *The Scythe*; and he is contributing co-editor of two anthologies: *Ki: Khanga: The Anthology* and *Steamfunk.*

Finally, Balogun is the Director and Fight Choreographer of the Steamfunk feature film, *Rite of Passage*, which he wrote based on the short story, *Rite of Passage*, by author Milton Davis.